MW01286569

Ghosted

by

Lori Matsourani

Cover Art by *The Wild Rose Press, Inc.*

The Wild Rose Press, Inc.
PO Box 708
Adams Basin, NY 14410-0708
Visit us at www.thewildrosepress.com

Publishing History
First Edition, 2025
Trade Paperback ISBN 978-1-5092-6254-0
Digital ISBN 978-1-5092-6255-7

Published in the United States of America

Dedication

To Kurt, my soul mate.
Nothing is missing when I'm with you.

Chapter 1: What's Nick Dorsey Doing Here?

The wedding was off.

Bethany Hendren steered the rental car over the Chesapeake Bay Bridge, her fingers clenching the wheel as she drove eastbound toward Maryland's Eastern Shore and her final destination—Worthington Cove. The sweep of water below the two-lane span sparkled as undulating swells reflected the setting sun. Only ten more miles to go before she could stop, allow herself to think, and fully embrace the fact that she was done with him.

Coming here was a spur-of-the-moment decision, made amid tears and a bottle of cabernet after she'd discovered Owen's secret. She'd been blindsided—never imagining he could be capable of doing that to her or she'd be oblivious when it happened. But here she was, reeling from the reality that her fiancé—make that *ex*-fiancé—was a philanderer. And a liar.

When she'd confronted him with evidence that his relationship with Kayla went beyond coworkers, his admission had left her nauseous and woozy. Now, after a five-hour flight from Oklahoma City to Baltimore, and another hour of driving, she'd progressed from shell-shocked to seething. She'd trusted him, and he'd betrayed her.

Her plan was to sort through everything with Aunt Ginny, who always knew the right thing to do when emotions threatened to override rational thought. With Aunt Ginny's help, she'd keep a level head and stick to her decision that Owen was not worth her forgiveness—or a second chance.

But Aunt Ginny didn't know she was coming, because Bethany hadn't told her, or anyone else, about the breakup.

The welcome sign for Worthington Cove came into view and she took comfort in the rows of familiar, colonial-era houses while navigating the town's streets. Ten years had passed since Bethany last visited her aunt and this small Kent Island town. But many childhood visits had stamped the route into her memory. She followed Main Street until she saw the State Street signpost, then turned right and guided the car down the cobblestone-paved road to Horatio House, the town's historic bed-and-breakfast.

She'd wanted to stay here since its renovation several years ago, envisioning it as the perfect destination for a romantic getaway. Except her love life was in ruins, so the centuries-old plantation house would be a hideaway instead, a neutral place where she could manage her anger, discard the humiliation, and move forward unencumbered.

Dusk had taken hold, but the inn's porch lights banished the shadows with their gentle glow. After unloading her luggage, Bethany paused to admire the stately house. Six tall pillars supported the front porch, which spanned the exterior's entire width. Dark shutters flanked the windows on the first and second floors, and three dormer windows jutted from the top floor's gambrel roof. The place was grand, a stark contrast to what she remembered when visiting as a kid—a dilapidated hulk with boarded windows, peeling paint, and an overgrown lawn.

Bethany grabbed her suitcase, climbed the front steps, and opened the door. Inside, the scent of cinnamon and baked apples greeted her as she took in the entryway's polished hardwood floor, gleaming from the soft light of a crystal chandelier. Beyond the foyer, several beige sofas and upholstered wingback chairs formed a casual seating area in front of a brick fireplace. The effect was comfortable and welcoming, like she'd stepped into a larger version of Aunt Ginny's cozy living room. And for the first time since downing the wine, booking the plane ticket, and reserving a room, it didn't hurt when she took a breath.

As she made her way to the front desk—an antique writing table by the stairs—an elegant gray-haired woman walked into the foyer and stopped, breathing in a quiet gasp when she saw Bethany. After staring for several seconds, the woman recovered and smiled warmly.

"Hi! You must be Ms. Hendren. Welcome to Horatio House. I'm Margaret Snowden, the innkeeper."

"Please call me Bethany."

"Bethany it is, then. Your room is ready." Mrs. Snowden selected an envelope lying on the desk and handed it to her, then tapped the vintage call bell. "I put you in the Howard Room, upstairs to the right. My nephew will carry your luggage up."

Bethany glanced at the staircase, admiring its graceful curve. "This house is lovely."

"Thank you, dear. We think so, too."

As Mrs. Snowden spoke, a tall, dark-haired man entered the foyer. He wore jeans and a soft blue crewneck sweater that accentuated his lanky, yet solid, build. As soon as he saw Bethany, his face lit up.

"Bethany!"

He walked toward her as though they were long-lost friends, and she half expected him to pull her into an embrace. Then she recognized the dark chocolate eyes behind the black-framed glasses and her stomach lurched.

Nick Dorsey. He's Mrs. Snowden's nephew?

"Aunt Margaret told me you were checking in today."

Stunned, Bethany stepped backward, bumping into the edge of the desk as her heart thudded. A white-hot flush scorched every inch of her skin as she stared at Nick. Of all the people she could run into, it had to be the first guy to break her heart? And why did he have to be so handsome, with that bit of hair curling over his forehead and late-day stubble?

She inhaled deeply to rein in her composure, hating her can't-catch-your-breath reaction to him, then dipped her chin in a neutral acknowledgment.

"Hello, Nick."

His smile morphed into a full-on, lopsided grin. "It's been ages since I've seen you. Ten years, I bet. Not since the summer Zach and I got our drivers' licenses."

Mrs. Snowden laid her hand on Nick's shoulder. "Bethany is staying in the Howard Room. Can you help her with her bag?" Then, turning to Bethany, she said, "Come back down when you're ready and I'll give you a tour of the house."

As Bethany followed Nick to the second floor, the pain, questions, and self-doubts she'd buried years ago reemerged, seeping into her belly like liquid concrete.

The last thing she needed was Nick Dorsey invading her healing zone. It had taken her months to get over the summer romance they'd shared—and he'd abruptly ended—when they were teens. And even longer before she could bring herself to date again.

And now he was in her safe space.

His gaze swept her face as they walked along the hallway, his demeanor openly curious. "Do you remember this house? The place was an absolute wreck."

Bethany straightened, determined to remain aloof and unaffected by the depth of his eyes. "Yep. I recall quite a bit." *That you kissed me. Said you loved me. Promised that you'd keep in touch. Then nothing. Silence. Like I never existed.* "But I never thought you'd be working here."

"I help Aunt Margaret now and then, but I work for Maryland's Eastern Shore Conservation Group. I'm a marine scientist." He stopped midway down the hall and hovered by a door with a plaque that read "Howard Room."

"I'll never forget the day Zach and I dared you to climb over the fence to confront the ghost." He chuckled. "You walked right onto the rickety porch and banged on that old door. It was monumental." His eyes gleamed as his lips curved upward, and her heart floundered at the familiar expression.

That day was etched in her memory, too. It was early June, a week after she'd arrived in Worthington Cove to stay with Grandma and Grandpa Hendren for the summer. She'd spent the afternoon at the town beach with her cousins Martie and Zach, and Nick, Zach's best friend. Nick was different that year. The cute, nerdy kid she'd hung out with the previous summers had transformed into a drop-dead-gorgeous seventeen-year-old. And he'd been flirting with her!

On the way back to her grandparents' house, they'd all stopped by the rusted chain-link fence surrounding Horatio House—people in town called it the old haunted mansion back then—and Nick started teasing her. He told her a ghost lived inside and bet she didn't have the guts to knock on the door and see for herself. But she'd accepted the challenge, intending to prove to her cousins and him, mainly him, that she was unafraid. That she could hold her own when it came to that eerie house and, despite being sixteen, she was worthy of his respect.

"That was a long time ago. And as I recall, there wasn't any evidence to support your ridiculous notion that the house was haunted." *And the days of trying to impress you are long gone.*

"Not that day. Anyway, I'm glad you're back." He opened the door and motioned her inside the large room. A vintage wrought-iron bed, as well as a nightstand with a tray of wine, cheeses, and stemware, occupied the wall on her left. An enormous stone fireplace, with an antique painting of a woman mounted over the mantel, dominated the opposite side of the room.

Nick studied the portrait as he set down the suitcase, then peered at Bethany. "Oh, wow. You look just like her."

The woman, dressed in eighteenth-century garments, appeared to be about Bethany's age. They had the same oval face, narrow nose, chestnut-brown hair, and caramel eyes.

"I see the likeness," Bethany said. "Who is she?"

"One of the Worthingtons. I'm sure Aunt Margaret knows her name."

She stepped closer to study the centuries-old canvas and encountered a cold spot in the room. A shiver coursed through her. "Is this room always so chilly?"

He frowned. "Not usually. I'll check the thermostat."

Bethany hoisted her suitcase onto the bed, impatient to end this unwelcome encounter with Nick. Then, without thinking, she pivoted away from the mattress and almost collided with him. He threw out his hands to steady her, his face inches away as his fingers clutched her upper arms. His dark eyes locked on hers.

"I turned up the heat." He maintained his grasp and her breath caught as she stared back, captivated by the richness of his almost-black irises.

"Thank you."

"And there's something else."

"What's that?" Her heart pounded, sending a rush of blood to her ears. She couldn't look away. Was he going to apologize? Explain why he'd ghosted her after that summer?

"Even though the family completely redid the inside and outside of the house, the ghost still haunts this place."

That's what he wants to tell me?

With a sigh, she shook off his grip and stepped out of his reach, disappointed in him for dodging the chance to explain what happened back then and frustrated with herself for letting him get to her. She'd conquered her feelings for him a decade ago and was determined to squelch any residual heart flutters.

"If you're trying to spook me, it's not going to work."

Again he flashed the grin she'd fallen for so many

years ago. "I'm just giving you a heads-up. The ghost is harmless, but its presence can be creepy. And, for some reason, it becomes even more active around this time of year."

"I appreciate the warning, but I don't believe in ghosts."

"You may change your mind."

She eyed him, unconvinced. "I doubt it."

"Aunt Margaret and some of her guests have felt its presence in this house. I have, too."

"Then maybe it'll visit you."

"It might. Or it may decide to drop in on you." Smirking, he headed toward the door. "Just saying."

"I'll keep that in mind."

"Fair enough." He backed into the hallway. "I'll be stopping by in the morning before work. Aunt Margaret's pastry is the best in town, and her coffee isn't bad, either. If you need anything, you'll know where to find me."

She nodded, knowing there was absolutely nothing she'd need from Nick Dorsey, and shut the door.

****

While unpacking, Bethany mulled over her encounter with Nick. Damn him, and his handsome face and heart-stopping grin. She had no intention of finding him or requesting a single thing. Avoiding him was more like it, because succumbing to his charms was off the table. Her heart had endured enough bruises from untrustworthy men. She'd be impervious—like stone— to everything about him. No way he'd break through her impenetrable façade.

With renewed determination, she closed her suitcase and returned to the foyer.

Mrs. Snowden looked up from the desk and smiled. "I hope you like your room, dear."

"I do. It's just what I'd imagined. I'm so glad you had a vacancy at the last minute."

"There was a cancellation this week, so your timing is perfect." Mrs. Snowden closed her laptop and stood. "Can I show you around?"

Bethany followed the innkeeper. "When I was a kid, my parents brought me to Worthington Cove every summer to visit my grandparents. Riding my bike past this house was always on my to-do list back then."

"Nick said he knew you when he was in high school. Your parents are Cat and Erick Hendren, right?"

"Yes. They grew up here, and my aunt, Ginny Jenkins, still lives in town. Apparently, my family's lineage goes back to Isabella Worthington. My grandfather on my mother's side, Joseph Day, was proud of our family's deep roots here."

"Ah, it makes sense, then. Your resemblance to the portrait in the Howard room."

"Is she Isabella?"

"No, that's Isabella's daughter, Ariella. I was quite surprised when you first walked in. The similarity is startling. For a moment, I thought you were an apparition." She paused, glancing at Bethany. "The house *does* have its ghost, you know."

Bethany responded with a snort. "Nick made sure to point that out."

"He does like to brag about our ghostly guest. But its presence—a sudden wisp of cold air, the faint scent of pipe tobacco, or a soft whisper—is more intriguing than intimidating."

"Did Ariella live here?"

"She did, with her husband, Frederick Howard. That's why we call your room the Howard Room. There's also the Worthington Room, the Watts Room, and other rooms named after Worthington family members." Mrs. Snowden waved her hand toward the back of the foyer. "Here, let's start in the kitchen. It's my favorite part of the house."

After leading Bethany through the inn, Mrs. Snowden ended the tour in the library. An assortment of leather-bound volumes filled a built-in wooden bookshelf. On the adjacent wall, barrister bookcases flanked a brick fireplace, where a fire burned in the hearth.

Mrs. Snowden turned to leave. "If you're interested in the Worthington family history, there's probably information here that's not available at the public library. Feel free to borrow any book we have."

Bethany settled into one of the overstuffed leather armchairs in front of the fireplace, looking forward to some time to herself. The flames lurched and wobbled as she snuggled deeper into the cushions. The past two days had drained her energy, but not her resolve. Her relationship with Owen was over. Done. There was no chance of reconciliation, although he'd begged her to forgive him. And her decision to cancel the wedding remained firm.

Had Owen ever loved her? Or was it her status he had found appealing? He'd worked hard to cultivate his image and often told her they were an ideal match and a great team: him, an upcoming superstar in the Oklahoma City real estate business, and her, a high-profile development manager with the prestigious Manning-Ross Institute of Petroleum Technology. Her friends agreed. They were a model couple.

The hype had bedazzled her, and look how it had turned out. She might have been Owen's perfect fiancée, but he'd chosen someone else, someone who wasn't his "ideal" match, to keep on the sly. His deception had shattered her heart, dismantled her confidence, and destroyed her ability to trust.

Well, it was over now, and she was moving on. She deserved someone honest and faithful. A man who loved her for her and not her position in Oklahoma City's corporate sector.

Basking in the warmth from the blaze, she relaxed for the first time since she'd discovered Owen's affair. Horatio House offered exactly what she needed: a quiet place to think and figure out her future. Tomorrow she'd visit Aunt Ginny, then browse the inn's library to learn more about her doppelgänger, Ariella. It'd be a welcome distraction from the turmoil that had wreaked havoc on her life, as well as the unexpected encounter with Nick Dorsey.

Chapter 2: The Intruder

"Oh, thank god I've found you! I thought you'd left me."

A male voice pulled Bethany from a deep sleep.

She jolted upright and, in the dimness, saw a man at the foot of her bed. Her pulse rate skyrocketed as panic seized her throat, making it difficult to swallow. Instinctively, she reached for her phone on the nightstand, then remembered it was on the dresser, charging.

He stood in the shadows, studying her. "You're so beautiful." A mixture of pain and longing filled his voice. "I've missed you."

Shaking, Bethany pulled the quilts up to her chin. "I think you're in the wrong room." Her words came out thick and garbled as she glanced toward the doorway, trying to focus. Should she make a run for it? It would be easy to slide out of the bed and bolt for the door. Her stomach heaved as she played the scenario in her head. What if she couldn't get away fast enough? Would he grab her and pull her back? Then what? Would Mrs. Snowden hear her if she screamed? As she contemplated her next move, he spoke again.

"I was a fool. I know that now."

"We don't know each other," she said, scooting toward the side of the mattress so she could dash out of the room. "And I'd feel more comfortable if you left."

"I only wanted to be a good husband for you. And make you happy."

He thinks I'm his wife. She frowned. Maybe he'd wandered in by mistake, and was a guest who'd mistaken her for someone else. She must have forgotten to lock the door. The pounding in her chest eased, but she remained wary.

"Uh…you've made a mistake. This isn't your room and I'm not your wife."

"But…" He hesitated. "I'm confused, my love. Why do you rebuff me?"

The intruder took a step closer, and Bethany, now accustomed to the dimness, saw him more clearly. His clothes—knee-length pants with a button fly, and a loose, rumpled pullover shirt that tied at the neck—resembled a colonial costume worn during historical reenactments. Strands of dark hair had escaped the ponytail at the nape of his neck and formed a haphazard frame around his cheeks and chin. A massive stain marked the left side of his shirt. He looked as though he'd been in a fight. No wonder he seemed disoriented. Probably had one beer too many after his show.

"I don't know who you are, but you're not my husband." Just a few more inches to go, and then she'd be at the edge of the bed and out of the room. "And you really need to leave. Right now." She had no patience for drunks.

"Please, don't banish me." Distress accentuated his words. "I should have known that a liaison with him was never your intention. But when I saw him—"

Suddenly, the man was by her side, blocking her path to the door. His expression radiated anguish as he held her gaze.

"I'm trying to remember last night's events, but the particulars elude me. It's like a veil has blocked my memory and I can only see bits and pieces. You must tell me what happened."

Before she could react, he leaned down, clasped her exposed hand, and pulled her fingers to his rough, unshaven cheek. His touch, cold and clammy, sent a chill through her body that left her shivering and lightheaded. Uneasiness flooded her chest as she pulled away from his grasp and stifled the urge to scream. *Don't show fear. Stay calm.*

"I'm sorry, but I don't know what you're talking about. Like I said, you're in the wrong room, and you're confusing me with someone else." She grasped the quilt tighter and motioned her head toward the door. "And I want you to leave."

He paused and stared, unfocused, at the wall behind her. "I'd finished my ledgers for the evening and retired to our bedroom. You weren't there, so I went downstairs to find you."

A scowl touched his lips and his tone shifted, became indignant. "When I reached the doorway to the salon, I saw him. He was trying to embrace you. In my home! I admit my rage engulfed me, hammering my entire being with a fury that quashed all my rational thoughts."

He took a breath and shifted his eyes back to her. "The dastard! How dare he make advances toward you." He clutched Bethany's shoulder through the quilt, and a range of emotions—anger, disbelief, and fear—distorted his face. "Before I realized what I was doing, I'd wrapped my hand around the hilt of my hunting knife and wielded it, unsheathed. After that, the details are hazy."

Her pulse surged, and a shudder coursed through her. Why was he telling her this? She should have run for it. Grabbed her phone, left the room, and called for help. But she hesitated and now was trapped by a disheveled amnesiac who, at one point, possessed a knife. She burrowed under the quilts, her thoughts roiling. Could she distract him? Or convince him to leave?

"What else do you remember?" she asked.

He frowned and locked his gaze on her. "That I fully intended to stab him."

Her heart seized at his words, but she continued, not knowing what else to do. "Who did you want to stab?"

The man blinked, appearing surprised. "Why, Frederick Howard, of course."

Frederick Howard. Ariella's husband?

"He was staying here, and we were to sail to Annapolis the next day." He loosened his grip on her shoulder. "God help me. Did I kill him? Ariella, am I…am I a murderer?"

Ariella? He knows about my resemblance to the woman in the portrait.

Her fear faded as anger took over. This had to be a performance. An elaborate ruse. She was being spoofed, and the person most capable of pulling this off was Nick Dorsey. He'd made a point to tell her about the ghost. And also hinted that she might get a visit.

Bethany's head throbbed as she glowered at the man by her bed. "I don't know who you are, but this charade is over. Get out now before I call the police."

"Charade?" His face crumpled. "It's me. Samuel. How do you not recognize me? All I want is to make things right between us."

"Yeah, well, I don't see that happening. You're leaving. Now. And you can tell Nick I was *not* amused by his prank."

Now even more determined to get this man out of her room, she swung her legs over the side of the bed and gripped his arm. The frosty surface of his sleeve startled her as she guided him toward the door and pushed him into the hallway. Then, after locking the door and checking the deadbolt, she went back to bed.

Chapter 3: Who Is Samuel Watts?

The next morning, Nick Dorsey's voice floated up from the first floor as Bethany headed downstairs. Although determined to keep her feelings neutral, the thought of seeing him sent a jolt of irritation careening through her veins. What was he thinking when he sent one of his buddies to her room in the middle of the night to "haunt" her? Maybe he wanted her to leave, and that was his way of convincing her to check out. Well, she wasn't going anywhere.

"Good morning." His mouth curved into his familiar lopsided grin. "How was your first night in Horatio House? Any ghosts stop by?"

She snorted. *As if he didn't know.* "No ghosts."

Mrs. Snowden set a mug of coffee and a cinnamon roll in front of Bethany. "That's not surprising. Only a few guests have felt our spirit. Its presence is subtle."

Bethany slid into the chair across from Nick and eyed him. "But I did have an unusual encounter last night."

He shifted, moving closer, and frowned. "Did you see a mouse? They tend to come inside this time of year. I can set a trap."

"No mouse, but a man. He came into my room last night dressed like a colonist from the seventeen hundreds. He seemed confused, and I thought he might have been drinking. At first."

"What?" Nick straightened in his chair, his frown deepening. "Are you okay?"

"I'm fine. But you knew I would be, right? Because you planned the whole thing."

His brows shot up. "What are you talking about?"

Bethany glared at Nick. "Someone who knows about my resemblance to Ariella played a joke on me. Maybe to convince me that ghosts and spirits are real."

"Hold on. Who's Ariella?"

"Ariella Worthington Howard," Mrs. Snowden replied. "She's the woman in the portrait in the Howard Room."

"You saw that Ariella and I look alike. And you made a point of telling me the ghost is still here." Bethany leaned closer to Nick, infuriated. "Admit it. You pranked me. My visitor last night was your doing."

"Me?" His eyes grew wide as he shook his head. "I'll admit I'm good for a gag now and then, but there's no way I could have come up with a stunt like that."

"Yeah, right." Bethany smirked. The Nick she knew that summer could have easily pulled it off. He was always playing practical jokes on her and Martie.

"Honestly, I had nothing to do with your visitor."

Bethany saw concern in his expression. Could he be telling the truth? But if he hadn't orchestrated last night's visitor, then who was that man? She shuddered.

"What did he look like?" Nick asked. He turned to Mrs. Snowden. "Aunt Margaret, could he be a guest?"

After Bethany described the intruder, Mrs. Snowden shook her head. "Neither of our male guests fit that description." Unease lined her forehead. "This has never happened before. How could someone get inside the house and into her room?"

Nick pushed away from the table. "I'll check the locks on the doors. Aunt Margaret, will you call the police?"

"Wait." Bethany reached out and grabbed his forearm. "I was pretty tired when I went up to my room and may have left the bedroom door unlocked. Besides, the guy seemed harmless. Could he be a neighbor? Or an actor in a reenactment? He left without incident and I don't want to get him in trouble."

Mrs. Snowden frowned. "I doubt it. None of my neighbors fit the description you gave, and the town doesn't have any events scheduled for this time of year. The next one is the history festival in September."

"What did he say?" Nick asked, his voice soft. "Did he threaten you?"

"He wasn't menacing at all. Distraught is a better description. He called me Ariella and referred to me as his wife. And he said he may have murdered Frederick Howard." She looked at Mrs. Snowden. "Didn't you tell me Frederick Howard was Ariella's husband?"

"Fredrick Howard was Ariella's *second* husband. Her first husband was Samuel Watts."

Bethany paused. "The man in my room said he was Samuel."

"He did?" Mrs. Snowden studied her for a moment. "Is it possible you were dreaming?"

A dream? Was that what she'd experienced? Bethany hesitated, then shook her head. "I don't think so. My dreams are never that lifelike, and usually I've forgotten them by the time I wake up. But I remember everything from last night. It felt very real."

"You know, dear, there is another possible explanation." Mrs. Snowden glanced at Nick, then back at Bethany. "The man you saw was the apparition of Samuel Watts."

"What?" Bethany gaped at Mrs. Snowden, dumbfounded. Had she really suggested the man in her room was a ghost?

"Ghosts can communicate with us while we sleep. Especially when they're connected to the space we're occupying. It's very likely that Samuel is haunting you."

Bethany stifled a laugh. "Haunting *me*?" There had to be another explanation. The idea of being haunted by a spirit was completely farfetched. "Did Samuel even live in this house?"

"He did," Mrs. Snowden answered. "With Ariella, centuries ago. Around the time of the American Revolution. His portrait hangs in the Watts Room. Would you like to take a look? The room's vacant at the moment."

Bethany nodded. It wouldn't change her mind about ghosts and hauntings, but she *was* curious to see the painting of Ariella's first husband. She followed Mrs. Snowden up the stairs to the end of the hallway. As they entered the room, the innkeeper pointed to the painting over the fireplace.

"He was very handsome, don't you think?" Mrs. Snowden said. "Unfortunately, Samuel passed away at a fairly young age. He was lost at sea while sailing to Annapolis."

Bethany examined the portrait. With his white powdered wig and formal attire, the man in the painting looked quite different from the befuddled, unkempt person in her room. Still, there were some striking similarities between the two, like the square jaw, slender nose, prominent forehead, and thick, dark eyebrows.

With a start, she realized he resembled her cousin, Tyler Day.

"Well," Mrs. Snowden asked. "Does he look like the man you saw in your room?"

"It's hard to say for sure."

She leaned against the doorjamb for support, studying the man in the portrait. He could be a composed, cleaned-up version of her visitor. Maybe the whole encounter *had* been a dream. Most likely, Grandpa Day had mentioned Ariella and her first husband while conveying the Day family history during Bethany's childhood visits. And last night she'd formed an image of Samuel based on Tyler.

Although the whole dream experience left her mystified, one thing she knew for sure. Ghosts didn't exist, and she wasn't being haunted.

****

"So, now do you believe in ghosts?" Nick asked with a smirk.

Seated again at the kitchen table, Bethany sipped her coffee. "No." She glared at him. Would he ever stop with the ghost routine? "Apparently, I had a dream. A vivid one, but still just a dream. There's no other explanation."

"Oh, I don't know." Mrs. Snowden slid into the chair next to Nick. "Maybe it's Samuel's ghost that's been here all this time, and now he's attached himself to you. After all, you look like his wife."

Bethany swallowed a sigh. Their ghost theories were annoying and needed to be shut down.

"The man in my dream thought he killed Frederick Howard the night before their trip to Annapolis. Did Samuel murder Frederick?"

Mrs. Snowden's eyebrows shot up. "Definitely not.

I'm sure they both boarded the ship." She paused. "That information should be in one of the inn's historical journals. If you'll give me a minute, I can look it up."

Bethany and Nick followed Mrs. Snowden to the inn's library. She removed a hard-bound volume from a shelf and set it on the large writing desk. *The Worthington Family, Volume II* was stamped in gold on the cover. She flipped through the pages, her eyes flicking back and forth as she scanned their contents.

"Here." She pointed to the text of a letter addressed to Ariella Worthington Watts from Captain Beauregard Perry of the *Lady Eleanor*.

"There was a storm in the Chesapeake Bay on October 18, 1774, the day Frederick and Samuel sailed to Annapolis. The waves washed Samuel overboard, and they never recovered his body. According to the family records, Frederick Howard delivered the captain's letter to Ariella on October 20, 1774, so he was very much alive after Samuel disappeared." Mrs. Snowden stopped. "What's today's date?"

Bethany glanced at her watch. "October nineteenth. Why?"

"Yesterday was the anniversary of Samuel's death." Mrs. Snowden looked up, her eyes dancing with excitement. "I bet it's another reason his spirit is reaching out to you, Bethany."

Except his spirit was *not* reaching out to her. It was crazy to even think that was possible.

Bethany flashed Mrs. Snowden an apologetic smile. "I'm sorry, but I just can't believe I'm being haunted. I had a dream, and an unreliable one at that."

As they spoke, the room's temperature fell several degrees, enough for Bethany to sense a chill. "It must be getting colder outside." She rubbed her hands together. "I can feel it in here."

Mrs. Snowden was quiet for a moment, her face solemn as she shook her head and glanced at Nick. "That's not a draft, dear. It's the spirit who haunts this house."

Bethany stifled another sigh. She'd endured enough ghost talk for one day and her mind was about to combust. A quick look at the grandfather clock let her know the town library was open and Aunt Ginny, the librarian, should be there. More than anything else, she needed her aunt's sympathetic ear and one of her all-encompassing hugs.

"Okay, then." Bethany backed up to retreat. "I'm heading out to see my Aunt Ginny. Maybe she'll have additional information on Ariella and her husbands."

The library was several blocks away, and she looked forward to a quiet stroll to clear her head and calm her nerves. Bethany retrieved her jacket and started walking. Just as she reached the end of the inn's walkway, Nick's deep voice called out from behind her.

"Bethany, wait up."

Now what? She stopped and reactivated her courteous smile, intending to slam the lid on this encounter as quickly as possible.

"Your dream," he huffed, breathless from running after her. "I'd really like to hear more about it."

She continued walking. "It's not that interesting."

"I bet it is." He synchronized his steps to hers. "Let's talk about it later, over lunch. The cream of crab soup at Lindy's is amazing. I'll buy."

Lunch with Nick? Bethany's heart banged so loudly she was certain he heard it. The heartache she'd tamped down so many years ago came rushing back, and she wondered if he even remembered the promise he'd made and broken so long ago. It didn't matter. She was in Worthington Cove to heal from the wreckage caused by one liar, not to be swayed by the charm of another one.

"I appreciate your invitation, but it's been a long time since I've seen Aunt Ginny and I don't want to put a time limit on my visit." She sped up. Then, to her dismay, he matched her stride.

"How about dinner? There's a restaurant at Tilghman's Marina. The Bayside Dock. They have the best crab cakes on the island."

She stopped. "Why are you so intent on hearing about my dream? You'd never even heard of those people."

He shrugged. "Curiosity, I guess. I've always wanted to know more about the house's past inhabitants. Maybe Aunt Margaret's right and it's Samuel's ghost haunting the place."

She resumed her pace. "I'm really not interested in listening to more ghost theories. It's not my thing."

"Then we can talk about something else. Catch up. That's what friends do."

Friends? *Friends*? Didn't he realize their friendship ended when he gave her the silent treatment ten years ago?

"But we haven't been friends for a long time, Nick."

Silence. From the corner of her eye, she saw he had stopped. She hadn't meant for her words to sound so abrupt, and a twinge of regret gripped her.

He'd been welcoming. Friendly. So why did she still hold a grudge? They were just kids when he broke off contact. A decade had passed since then, and she'd moved on. The mature approach was to ask him about it. Find out what happened and be done with it. Dinner would give her an opportunity to broach the subject.

She faced him. "Okay, I'll tell you about the dream. Tonight, over crab cakes. But only if you promise not to bring up ghosts."

"Promise." He swiped at the hair flopping over his forehead and smiled. "I'll meet you at the inn at six. That sound good?"

"Sure."

Chapter 4: Why Not Give Nick a Chance?

Accepting Nick's invitation was a mistake. How could she sit across from him and pretend everything was okay? His silence years ago wasn't only a rejection of their romance. He'd shunned their friendship—the sacred alliance they'd formed while searching for sand crabs and building sand castles the summer she turned thirteen. It was supposed to keep them connected forever, and three years later, she'd still believed their bond could never be severed. Until Nick pulled away and tore apart everything between them.

Although Bethany had buried it deep, the hurt from his snub still lingered. And knowing why he'd ignored her would only exacerbate the old wound. The last thing she needed was a resurgence of teenage heartache. What happened in the past should stay in the past. Nick should stay in the past.

By the time she reached the local branch of the Queen Anne's County Public Library, housed in the historic Greenberry Mansion, Bethany knew she had to cancel dinner with Nick. She'd ask Mrs. Snowden for his number and send him a text. Then, bracing herself to tell Aunt Ginny about Owen, Bethany opened the library's heavy wooden door.

Inside, at the end of the foyer, she saw her aunt behind the ornate cherrywood counter, staring at a computer screen while twirling strands of gray/brown hair that had escaped her messy bun.

"Aunt Ginny!"

Ginny looked up and squinted at Bethany from behind a pair of wire-rimmed glasses. Then she stood and smiled.

"Bethany!"

Bethany blinked back tears as her aunt rushed across the foyer and folded her into an embrace. She held on, savoring the warmth of the hug and comfort from the presence of her mom's only sister. Although it'd been ten years since she'd seen Aunt Ginny in person, they'd stayed in touch with phone calls, video chats, and letters tucked into birthday and Christmas cards. Still, Bethany missed spending time with her aunt. She felt closer to Aunt Ginny than anyone else, even her mother.

"Oh, sweetheart, look at you." Aunt Ginny pulled away and studied her. "You're taller. And gorgeous, as always. I love your short haircut. Very chic."

Aunt Ginny led them to a polished wooden table. "What a wonderful surprise! I assumed you'd be busy planning your wedding and never imagined I'd get to see you before the big day. I would have gotten the guest room ready, but Cat didn't tell me you were coming. How long are you staying?"

"Just a week. And Mom doesn't know I'm here."

"Oh?" Aunt Ginny pushed her glasses up the bridge of her nose, her hazel eyes questioning. "Is everything okay?"

"No. Not really." Bethany swiped at the cascade of tears loosened by her aunt's question. "I broke up with Owen and canceled the wedding. I found out he was cheating on me."

"Oh, honey." Aunt Ginny moved to the chair next to

Bethany and wrapped an arm around her shoulders.

"I feel like such an idiot. Turns out he's not the man I thought he was." Bethany released a short, harsh laugh as she dabbed at her face with a tissue Aunt Ginny produced. "Apparently, when he said he loved me, it didn't mean the same thing to him as it did to me. At least I found out before the wedding."

"I'm here to listen if you need to talk."

Bethany leaned over and hugged her aunt. "I'm so glad I came. I can't imagine talking to anyone but you about this. Right now, though, I need time to process Owen's affair and figure out how to break it to Mom and Dad that I won't be marrying him. Ever."

"They'll understand, trust me." Aunt Ginny returned the embrace. "Your parents want you to be happy. We all do. And marrying the wrong man doesn't bode well for a happily ever after."

Bethany glanced down at her left hand. "I gave him the ring back. All it represented were lies and betrayal." She rubbed her thumb against the slight indent on her ring finger. "After that, I couldn't stomach the thought of running into him or anyone else in Oklahoma City. So I packed a suitcase and came here."

"Well, you can stay with me for as long as you want." Aunt Ginny started toward her desk. "We can drive over now. Get you situated. Where's your suitcase?"

"Thank you so much. I appreciate the offer. But…" Bethany reached out and touched her aunt's arm, stopping her. "I booked a room at Horatio House and checked in yesterday."

"What?" A slight frown touched Aunt Ginny's lips. "Are you sure you want to stay there? Alone?"

She nodded. "Now that it's renovated, the inn is the perfect place for me to get some time to myself so I can recalibrate my life."

"Still. The old mansion can be a bit…intimidating."

"Please don't worry. It'll be fine. It's nothing like the wreck it used to be."

Aunt Ginny frowned. "I'm sure it isn't, but Horatio House has a reputation for being haunted."

Haunted? Oh, Aunt Ginny. Not you, too.

Bethany smiled. "Yeah, I know. Mrs. Snowden told me. But I've stayed at haunted hotels before and never encountered a ghost. And I don't expect to see one at Horatio House."

"Well, if that's where you want to be, I won't try to change your mind." Sighing, Aunt Ginny returned to the table. "The inn can always use the support. It's a tourist draw, and lord knows we need tourists. Things have been rough for a lot of the town's small businesses since the pandemic. Still…" She grinned and patted Bethany's hand. "I'd rather have you at my house."

"I know, but I'd just be in the way. Besides, Horatio House isn't creepy at all. Mrs. Snowden gave me a tour yesterday, and the place is stunning inside. Like something out of a colonial home-and-garden magazine."

"I'm not surprised. Margaret Snowden goes to great lengths to keep it in pristine condition, and I'm very grateful that she does. Everyone expected the owners to tear it down. But they restored it instead, thank goodness. Losing Horatio House would have been a shame. Not only was the mansion built by our family's ancestors, but it also played a significant role in the town's history."

Bethany leaned toward her aunt. "How so?"

Aunt Ginny settled into her chair. "The town's origins go back to the tobacco farm Thomas and Isabella Worthington inherited around the middle of the eighteenth century. They added to the acreage, expanded the tobacco crop, and called the plantation Worthington's Cove since the land included a large creek that emptied into the Chesapeake Bay. They built the mansion as the family's residence and named it after Isabella's father, Horatio Ridgely."

"I didn't know Worthington Cove used to be a plantation."

"I uncovered the details while doing research for the town's upcoming history festival. Worthington's Cove was one of the larger plantations in Queen Anne's County, around eight hundred acres. Over the centuries, the land was parceled off to Thomas and Isabella's heirs, who built homes on their plots. The family community eventually became the town of Worthington Cove. In the early days, Horatio House often served as a meeting place for the town's residents."

Bethany nodded, acknowledging the sense of security she'd always felt when visiting Worthington Cove. Her roots—her heritage—were here.

"Do you know anything about Isabella's daughter, Ariella? Her portrait hangs over the fireplace in my room at the inn."

"I know we're directly related to her. She was the oldest of Isabella's four daughters." Aunt Ginny went to her desk and retrieved a worn, leather-bound book. "There should be more information on her in here." She flipped through the yellowed pages and stopped.

"Ariella married Samuel Watts, a landowner and tobacco grower in Queen Anne's County. Thomas and

Isabella gave them Horatio House, plus a portion of the surrounding land, as her dowry. Ariella and Samuel had three daughters. Mary, Sarah, and Catherine." She looked up. "We're Catherine's descendants." Aunt Ginny adjusted her glasses and leafed through more pages. "Samuel perished at sea in 1774. After Samuel's death, Ariella married Frederick Howard."

Bethany absorbed the information. The town's historical records corroborated the inn's information about Frederick Howard. Obviously, her subconscious had invented Samuel's knife fight and Frederick's murder.

"Are there any other details about Samuel's death?" Bethany asked.

Aunt Ginny thumbed through the rest of the book. "No. I'm sorry, hon. Not in here. Is there something specific you're looking for?"

"No. Just curious about our ancestors. Mrs. Snowden thinks I look like Ariella."

"Really?" Aunt Ginny looked up, her hazel eyes bright. "We have another reference book that includes several Worthington family portraits." She darted into an adjacent room and returned with a thicker leather-bound volume. Her fingers quickly flicked through the book before stopping on a color reproduction of the painting in the Howard Room. Aunt Ginny raised her gaze and studied Bethany, then refocused on the page.

"Lord almighty. This could be you in the painting. The resemblance is uncanny."

"It's weird, right? Makes me want to find out everything I can about her."

Aunt Ginny turned several pages. "There's not much more on Ariella, only that Catherine and her husband Benedict Dorsey inherited Horatio House when Ariella passed away."

"Catherine married a Dorsey?" Bethany interrupted, her voice catching in her throat. "Are we related to Nick Dorsey?" The words slipped out before she could stop them.

"Margaret Snowden's nephew?" Aunt Ginny looked up and smiled. "I'm sure we are, hon. We probably share distant relatives with most of the locals here. Don't worry, though. If you and Nick have an ancestor in common, that person lived over two hundred years ago, which would make you and Nick…let's see…fifth or sixth cousins, or thereabout." She shot Bethany a full-fledged grin. "Why do you ask? Have you run into him?"

Although relieved their family connection was distant, Bethany silently scolded herself. Why would she care? The romance between them ended long ago.

"He was at Horatio House when I checked in."

"I knew he helped Margaret with the inn. How is he? You two were best friends when you were kids."

"He invited me out for crab cakes tonight at the marina. But I don't know if having dinner with him is such a good idea."

Aunt Ginny studied her. "I think it's a great idea. Dinner out with an old friend might do you a world of good."

Bethany hesitated, debating on how much to share. Although her past friendship with Nick hadn't been a secret, she'd never divulged the details of their relationship with her aunt. And she hadn't admitted to anyone that he'd gone silent when she returned home, or that it left her hurt and bewildered. She'd kept it to herself, hiding the snub along with the pain.

"Remember that summer I spent here with Grandma and Grandpa Hendren? When I was sixteen?"

She chuckled. "Yep. And you and Nick were thick as thieves. Whenever I saw you, he was right by your side."

Bethany's cheeks flushed as she remembered the night they kissed by the fountain at Ridgely Park—her first romantic kiss. "I had a crush on him back then."

"Oh, honey, everyone knew you two had a thing for each other."

"I felt like I was in love, and I thought he was, too. On my last night here, we sat on the town beach, just the two of us. He asked me to be his girlfriend. Promised to text me every day and said we'd video chat once a week. I was over-the-moon happy about it." Bethany held her aunt's gaze, her chest heavy with the memory. "And then…nothing. I went back home and never heard from him again."

A frown touched Aunt Ginny's forehead. "That doesn't sound like Nick."

"Well, that's what happened, and it broke my heart."

"I'm sure it did, but that was a long time ago. Nick's grown up since then, and so have you." Aunt Ginny tucked an arm around Bethany. "Besides, it's only dinner. Why not give him a chance?"

Should she? Their summer romance had been nothing more than puppy love, and before yesterday, she hadn't given him a thought for years. What was the worst that could happen? That she would try the best crab cakes on the island? Find out what happened and finally put Nick's brush-off to rest? Be friends again?

"You're right. Why not?"

****

Bethany left the library and wandered down State Street instead of going back to the inn. The town's historic district was bustling, with cars and small trucks filling the single-lane road and pedestrians hurrying past her.

She passed a row of narrow brick townhouses, many converted into quaint boutiques and offices, and stopped at The Toasted Bean coffee shop in the last house on the block. Bethany ordered a mocha latte to go, then crossed the street into Ridgely Park.

In the midmorning sun, maple and oak trees cast dappled shadows onto a brick pathway that wound through the small pocket park. She spotted the ornate cast-iron fountain standing in the center of the grounds and settled into a bench in front of it—the same bench she'd shared with Nick so long ago. She sipped her latte, watching the water cascade down the sculpture, and found her thoughts drifting back to the night he first kissed her.

It was mid-July, and she'd spent the afternoon swimming and sunning on the town beach with Nick, Zach, and Martie. Nick was taller that summer, more muscular, and unusually flirty with her. They were friends, but that day it'd felt like more. He'd rubbed sunscreen onto her back when they sat on blankets in the sand, wrapped his arm around her waist as they walked through the surf, and grabbed her hands to pull her into the waves. Her senses had thrummed while her brain etched every touch into her memory.

The outing ended at Verrazano's for colas and pepperoni pizza. The group had grabbed the back booth and Nick slid into the spot next to her, sitting so close that his thigh and hip pressed against hers.

She'd thought her heart would burst when he'd grasped her hand under the table and intertwined their fingers as though it were the most natural thing in the world to do. The warmth of his touch felt strangely intimate, as though they'd crossed a threshold into something beyond friendship. Her skin sizzled and her limbs buzzed, new sensations that elevated her feelings for Nick Dorsey to a whole new level.

When they'd left Verrazano's, he draped his arm around her shoulders and offered to walk her back to her grandparents' house. "Let's stop at the Ridgely Park fountain on the way," he'd said. "I have a dime and want to make a wish."

They'd strolled as one toward the park, their footsteps in sync, hips touching, and arms circling each other's waist. The town's streetlights illuminated the dark evening sky, and strains of a popular love song drifted out of Ridgely's Tavern. Nick sang along softly, pausing occasionally to brush his lips against the top of her head. She'd leaned in and pulled him even closer, savoring the warmth of his body against hers in the cool night air.

The fountain that night was magical. Spotlights positioned at the edges of the narrow brick patio lit the cast-iron maiden as she filled her goblet from an urn with a never-ending flow of water. Nick stopped and retrieved his dime. Bethany fished a penny out of her pocket, and they counted to three before flinging their coins into the pool.

After settling on a nearby bench, he drew her into his arms. Was this it? The moment she'd wondered about, waited for? She looked up into his eyes and inhaled, filling her lungs with the scent of sunscreen and salty air. His scent. Then he leaned down, touched her cheek with his index finger, and brushed his mouth against hers. His lips, spiced with traces of red pepper flakes, were softer than she had imagined. Without thinking, she lifted her face to his, hungrily snatching more kisses until she'd spent her last breath.

"My wish came true," he'd murmured, tightening his arms around her as his mouth rested on hers.

She'd whispered back, "So did mine."

The memory dredged up the old ache, now muted by time. Nick thought they were still friends, although he'd been the one who ended their relationship. Was it possible he still thought about her, and his heart still pounded with the chemistry that had pulled them together so long ago?

She gulped the rest of her latte. It was pointless to speculate. Her plan was to forge a path forward, not relive the past. They'd been teenagers exploring a first crush, and his silence had destroyed it. Since then, she'd buried her heartache, grown up, and moved on.

So why was she even thinking about him?

Dealing with the fallout from Owen's infidelity was hard enough, and mixing in revived feelings for Nick would be catastrophic. Emotional self-destruction. She needed to avoid rekindling any sort of friendship with Nick. It was the key to getting her heart, and her life, back on track.

After locating a loose quarter in her purse, she tossed the coin into the shimmering, sunlit pool. Then, looking up at the maiden, she whispered, "Please help me be strong."

Chapter 5: Crab Cakes at the Marina

At the restaurant, Nick guided Bethany to a table on the dockside patio and sat across from her. Behind his black-framed glasses, deep brown eyes reflected the glow from the overhead party lights, creating the illusion of sparkling pools of dark water that threatened to wash away all of her coherent thoughts. She inhaled the cool, briny air to regain control of her senses, and shivered.

"Are you cold?" he asked. "We can move inside."

"Thanks, but I'm fine out here." She studied the menu, a handy distraction until the server stopped at their table.

"Ready to order?" Nick raised his brow. "You want the crab cakes, right?"

"If they're the best on the island, I don't think I have a choice."

He laughed. "And beer, too? How about a pitcher? They have a local pale ale on tap that's pretty good."

"Sure." She surveyed the view of the bay as he spoke to the server. A sliver of the sun, barely visible above the horizon, painted both the sky and water with brilliant hues of pink and purple. In the distance, headlights of vehicles crossing the Bay Bridge lit up its length, creating the illusion of two sparkling ribbons stretched over the inky bay.

"I'd forgotten how much I love it here," she said. "Sitting by the water is peaceful. And so calming. I don't do it very often."

"You don't get to the shore much?" he asked.

"Hardly ever. It's too far away."

"You still live in Oklahoma, then?" His eyes remained on her.

She dipped her chin in acknowledgment, surprised he remembered. "Oklahoma City. Well, in a suburb about a half hour north of the city's business district. But I work in town."

"A city girl." He grinned and settled into his chair. "What kind of work takes you there?"

He smiled, his upper lip forming its crooked curve, just as it had when they were teens. And it affected her the same way it had all those years ago: her heart thumped and her cheeks flamed.

Ugh, dinner out with an old friend was *not* doing her a world of good. She grasped her dinner napkin and twisted it, hoping to dispel her unease and block the nervous chatter that threatened to take over. But it didn't work.

"For the past four years, I've worked for the Manning-Ross Institute of Petroleum Technology. As the director of development." Her fingers wrestled with the paper napkin in her lap. "It's a fancy corporate term for a fundraiser. My job is to plan programs and events that keep donations coming in from the institute's sponsors and donors."

He nodded, his gaze steady. She continued twisting. "The institute always needs money, so my work is never done."

"I wondered why you haven't been back."

His expression, warm and inviting, sent her thoughts to the last summer they'd spent together and the soft caress of his lips as he kissed her.

Be strong. Be strong. Be strong.

"Bethany?"

His voice brought her back to the present. She glanced down to avoid his eyes. The napkin was now a shredded heap in her lap, and more heat found its way to her face. To cool the burn in her skin, she sipped water and looked toward the marina's twin piers with rows of sailboats extending into the bay. Then she refocused on him.

"I'm sorry. What did you say?"

"It's been a long time since I've seen you in Worthington Cove."

"I haven't been back here since I was sixteen, the summer we all hung out together."

"Why not? You used to visit all the time during summer vacations."

"We stopped coming after my father's parents passed away. They were the main reason my mom and dad kept coming to visit, and it just wasn't the same without them." *And I couldn't risk seeing you again.*

"I get it." His smiled dimmed. "It's hard when you lose family members. But I'm surprised your parents stopped coming."

"My mom and dad were never fans of small-town life. As soon as they graduated from high school, they got married and moved to Oklahoma City. Coming back during the summer was more of a family obligation than a vacation for them. But I always liked the slower-paced shore vibe here."

"I like it too, even though it can get pretty quiet around here." He paused when the server set down the pitcher and two frosted mugs, then poured a glass for each of them. "But why Oklahoma City?" he continued. "I mean, other cities are closer. Like Baltimore or DC. Even Philadelphia."

"I don't know." She shrugged. "Opportunity, maybe. My dad went to college there, got a petroleum engineering degree, then took a job with an oil company in Oklahoma City. But I don't think they ever really fell in love with the place. My dad landed a new job in Florida a few years ago, and now they live in Jacksonville."

"So, no family left in Oklahoma City?"

She shook her head. "None."

"But you still have family in Worthington Cove?"

"My dad's brother Steve, and his wife Kim."

"Zach and Martie's parents, right?"

"Yes. And Aunt Ginny, of course. My mom's sister. She's the town librarian. Her daughter—"

"Is Sarah."

"You know her?"

He chuckled. "Of course. This is a small town. Everybody knows everybody."

"That's one of the things I love about Worthington Cove. It's much more personal than the city. I don't know why my mom and dad ever wanted to leave this place."

His face turned somber. "Knowing everyone has its downside."

"Really? Why?"

"Privacy is hard to come by. The whole town knows your business, and sometimes people try to get more involved in it than they should."

"Oh." She studied him, surprised by the observation. "Did something hap—"

As she started to ask him for details, the server arrived with baseball-size crab cakes. Bethany eagerly dug in, her food upstaging the question for Nick.

"Wow." She pointed at the plate with her fork. "This is good. I've missed Maryland crab cakes."

A smile pulled at his lips as he poked at his plate. "Told you they were the best. So what brought you back to town after all this time, besides our amazing seafood?"

Bethany hesitated. There was no reason to tell him about her broken engagement. She wanted him to see her as a successful career woman, able to navigate the world on her terms, and immune to relationship heartache.

"I wanted a change of scenery." A reasonable explanation, and very true. "Worthington Cove holds a special place in my heart, and I missed it." Also true.

"A change, huh?" He rested his wrists on the table, cutlery in hand, and eyed her with friendly curiosity, as though he was expecting her to disclose every detail that prompted her to take some time off. Is that what people did in small towns? Wait patiently with an affable grin until they harvested every tidbit of information out of you?

She nodded, intending to reveal as little as possible. "Oklahoma is landlocked, you know. It's a prairie. No seashore within five hundred miles."

"Sounds torturous. I bet you're relieved to be here. We're much closer to the beach."

"I am, actually. The fast pace of the city can be exhausting. It was time to move into the slow lane for a while." That wasn't a complete lie. She *had* jumped off the wedding track, reducing all activity in that lane to a permanent stop.

"Well, you couldn't have picked a better place to

stay. Since its restoration, Horatio House is the nicest bed-and-breakfast in town. Actually, it's the best on the whole island." Nick stabbed at a French fry with his fork, and his eyes flashed with mischief. "Even though it's haunted."

"As you mentioned yesterday. Is that why you want to know more about my dream? Because your aunt thinks I'm being haunted by a ghost?"

"It's not that far-fetched, you know." He pushed at the sprig of dark hair hovering near his eyebrow. "Spirits reach out to us while we're asleep."

"I see," she replied. "And you know that because a spirit contacted you in a dream?"

"Uh…no. But that's irrelevant because we're talking about *your* dream." He watched her expectantly.

"Hold on. If I recall, a condition of this dinner was no ghost talk."

"I kept my word. You're the one who said the g-word." The crooked grin took hold as he sat back and folded his arms with a confidence that was almost smug, like he knew he'd won the current round of tug-of-war and wanted to make sure she acknowledged it. "But I would like to hear more about your dream."

As she observed him, the past came rushing back. A younger version of Nick slouched in a beach chair, cheeks sunburned and hair tousled from the wind, beaming after a debate over something trivial.

Those moments had usually ended in an embrace.

She glanced down at her plate, dodging his gaze. It would be so easy to get sucked into a time warp and resurrect those old feelings for him. But her infatuation had led to a romantic crash-and-burn, something she had no intention of repeating. She was here to heal from

Owen's deception and get on with her life. Falling for Nick Dorsey again was not an option.

"Okay." She'd keep her end of the bargain but avoid eye contact. "A deal is a deal."

He scooped up a forkful of crab. "So, tell me everything."

Bethany described the encounter with Samuel between bites of her entrée, emphasizing the parts of his story that differed from historical records. Nick listened intently without discussion, interrupting several times to ask a question or two. By the time she completed her narrative, each had finished their meal.

"What's next?" he asked. "More family research?"

She folded her hands over the shredded bits of napkin piled in her lap. "Probably. But I also want to visit the town's shops and historic buildings, and maybe read a book or two. I'm keeping my schedule open."

She glanced up, caught his eye, and he shot her a grin, raising his brows above his glasses just enough to give him an impish look. Her breath hitched in response, and she silently cursed her fluttering heart for reacting to him like a smitten sixteen-year-old.

"Ready to head back to the inn?" he asked.

"Sure." Bethany swallowed, grateful they were leaving before those pesky feelings for him overwhelmed her. She pointed to her empty plate as she stood. "By the way, these crab cakes totally exceeded my expectations."

****

As they walked back to the inn, Bethany counted on the shadows from the street lamps to mask Nick's probing gaze and boost her courage to ask him what happened all those years ago. His reason might help her find closure and make peace with the past. And then, maybe, they could part as friends.

But what if his explanation inflicted a fresh wound instead?

She hesitated, and Nick broke the silence. "There's something captivating about this town at night. It gives me a sense of anticipation, like something exciting is just ahead."

"It's the same for me, too," she replied, relieved her question remained unasked. "Like anything is possible, as though the darkness dismantles all the barriers we erect during the day."

He turned his head. "Are there specific barriers you're referring to?"

Fear. She was afraid to find out what happened that summer. And truth. Did she really want to know why he'd ghosted her?

As she contemplated a reply, his fingers brushed against hers. She stiffened, surprised by his touch and flustered by the warmth of his skin. Immediately, her mind went blank, his question and her reply obliterated by the rapid thudding inside her chest.

Be strong.

"I'm sorry," she mumbled, moving her hand away from his to scratch her cheek, then fidget with her purse strap. "What did you say?"

His voice carried a hint of amusement. "I'm curious to know about the barriers you've erected. What are they?"

"Nothing in particular." She paused, collecting her thoughts. "There's something about the night that makes me want to let go of my daytime inhibitions and embrace life. To take risks and try something new. Enjoy what's ahead."

"In that case, why don't we take a detour? Walk down Main Street and have a nightcap at Ridgely's Tavern. Have you ever been there?"

"I don't think so."

"Perfect. A new experience for you, then. It's one of the oldest taverns on the Eastern Shore. People say it's haunted."

She glanced up at him and snorted. "There you go again. Bringing up ghosts."

A cocky smirk touched his mouth as he watched her. She recognized it as the same expression he'd often worn that summer. It was a reminder that he was still the same Nick she fell for years ago. But the Nick standing next to her now was a seasoned version of that boy. He'd grown up, matured, and become even more appealing.

He stopped next to a street lamp and turned toward her. "Guilty as charged. But I'm told the ghosts there tend to be elusive. So what do you think? Are you up for it?" The soft yellow light illuminated his face, emphasizing the hypnotic depth of his dark eyes.

Bethany chewed the inside of her lip, battling the spark that warmed her entire body. Grown-up Nick was a very charming man, and spending more time with him was tempting. As she acknowledged her attraction to him, a familiar sting pricked her ribs. He'd hurt her before. Did she really want to give him the power to do it again?

"I should get back to the inn, but please don't end your evening because of me." She forced a smile. "Why don't you go. And if you see one of those elusive ghosts, tell it I said hello."

"But—"

"And thanks again for dinner. It was an amazing treat. Goodnight."

Bethany retreated, almost running down the block until she saw State Street, then rushed toward Horatio House. Leaving Nick standing alone on the street was spineless, and she hated that she'd done it. But what choice did she have?

****

The inn resonated with a quiet stillness as Bethany climbed the stairs to her bedroom. What was she thinking, dashing off and leaving Nick? All he'd suggested was a drink. And her response, that abrupt, gutless exit, might have been—no, it definitely was—rude.

She grabbed the bottle of merlot from the nightstand, along with the Worthington family history book she'd borrowed from the inn's library, and climbed into bed. Not bothering with a glass, she gulped a mouthful of wine from the bottle and flipped through the book's pages. But the text flitted by, ignored. Her thoughts kept circling back to Nick.

He deserved an apology.

His invitation was a sociable gesture between friends, nothing more. So why had she panicked? One drink wouldn't set her up for heartbreak. Her emotions were under control and she'd make sure they stayed that way. Spending time with him wouldn't be an issue.

Satisfied with her decision, Bethany set the wine bottle and the history book on the nightstand, turned off the lamp, and snuggled under the heavy covers. Tomorrow, she'd make amends.

Chapter 6: It's Just a Dream

Sounds—rhythmic thuds, like someone walking across a wooden floor in sturdy boots—plucked at Bethany's brain. She cracked an eye open and saw Samuel, dressed as before, pacing her room. His presence sent her pulse soaring.

Stay calm. You're dreaming.

She gulped a mouthful of icy air and pulled the quilts up to her chin. He continued to pace, shuffling back and forth alongside the bed, his brow furrowed in concentration. Then he stopped and fixed his gaze on her. An anguished, low-pitched sigh escaped his lips.

"Ariella."

The intensity of his stare was mesmerizing, and she blinked to break its hold.

Don't let him get to you. It's just a dream. He isn't real.

"I told you before. I'm not Ariella."

"The night Howard and I fought… I recall a bit more now, but the details are frustratingly elusive. It's like they're shadowy figures, lurking just beyond the images I've managed to salvage." He continued to focus on her, his stare intense and searching. "Why can't I remember them?"

"I don't know, and I can't help you. So please. Leave me alone." Shivering, Bethany turned away from him and burrowed deeper beneath the covers. She had nothing to offer that could ease his pain.

More footsteps. The dull thumps circled her bed and stopped. She lifted an eyelid, barely opening it halfway, and gasped. Samuel's face floated above hers, his eyes wide and pleading as he peered down at her.

"You must help me reconstruct what happened. You were there."

Her patience with this dream—and this man—was dwindling. "No. I wasn't."

He leaned in, hovering so close she saw a tiny clump of dirt clinging to the stubble on his cheek. The scent of lavender mixed with pipe tobacco surrounded him. "The scuffle with Howard. I recall swiping at him with my knife, and the blade caught his arm. That wound shouldn't have been fatal, and I don't remember inflicting another."

He paused, looking upward as though scouring his memory. "I don't believe I murdered him. However, something else happened. I'm trying to grasp what it was, but it's circumventing my recollection." His attention returned to her. "How did we resolve our skirmish?"

His gaze grew intense and unwavering as he loomed above her, and irritation tweaked her nerves. He was invading her space, and she was ready for this dream to end.

She scowled. "For god's sake, listen to me. I don't know what happened that night. I wasn't there. And I'm not Ariella." She turned away, tugging the quilts up to her neck, and shut her eyes. "But I *do* know you didn't murder Frederick Howard. And I want you to leave my room. Now. You're interrupting my sleep and it's extremely annoying."

The mattress shifted. Did he just sit on the edge of her bed? She groaned, her annoyance provoked into full-on exasperation, and pushed him with her foot. The impact was hard.

"You. Need. To. Go."

Instead of leaving, he moved closer, hovering over her until his breath, dry and wintry, brushed her cheek. She cringed, unnerved by the sensation, then peeked through her eyelashes.

He was only inches away from her. *Ugh.* She quickly slid away from him and sat up, yanking the quilt as close as possible to her chin. More than anything, she wanted this to be over. Then, shooting him a fierce glare, she shouted. "Oh, my god! Can you please just leave me the hell alone?"

He winced. "Ariella." His voice wavered as moisture collected in the corner of his eye. "Please don't…"

Dammit. She'd brought him close to tears. Bethany sighed, stung by a twinge of guilt, and decided to hear him out. Once he'd said his piece, maybe this dream would end, and she'd get some rest.

"Okay. Let's recap what you remember. You got into an altercation with Frederick after you found him with Ariella, and you pulled out your knife and cut his arm."

He straightened and nodded. "Yes."

"Why was he in your home? Were you expecting him?"

"I hadn't anticipated Howard's arrival that day." He paused, frowning at the floor, then lifted his chin. "He asked me to accompany him to a meeting in Annapolis. It was a political gathering. Something to do with British tea. We were going to sail out together the next day. The closest lodging was miles away in Broad Creek, near the ferry. So I invited him to stay the night as our guest, despite my instincts to send him to the inn."

"Do you remember the date?"

"Only that it was mid-October, after the fall tobacco harvest. I was too busy to leave the plantation, but Howard was insistent. He said it was important for us as colonists to stand together against the English Parliament. I took him at his word and agreed to attend."

"What happened after that?"

"Later that evening, I…" He exhaled a choked breath. "I found him with his arms around you." His eyes closed for a long moment, as if to block the memory. "I remember coming into the salon and finding him there with you. I couldn't bear it. The audacity! How could he ever think it was his right to force such intimacy upon another man's wife? The man abused my hospitality and betrayed my trust."

"Okay. You've already established he was acting out of line."

Samuel recoiled. "But your virtue was at stake, as was my honor. I had no other course of action but to draw my blade."

"You said you intended to stab him. I'm assuming there was a struggle when you sliced his arm."

His lips trembled before pressing into a grimace. "Yes. I saw him looming over me with the knife in his hand. His face was so close I could feel his breath. He smelled of wine. And then he sneered at me, a victor's taunt, just before…" Samuel stopped, distress contorting his features as his eyes clamped shut.

"Before what, Samuel?"

His eyelids flew open, his gaze wild and aimless. "I felt a hot, searing explosion within me. The pain was all-consuming and I…I…" His body shook as he stared, unseeing, at the wall behind her.

"Samuel, look at me," she commanded, struggling to keep her voice from breaking. How could she conjure up such a cruel scenario for this man? Still, she pressed on, unable to let it go. "Tell me what he did."

A sob choked his words, and he gasped for air. "He stabbed me, Ariella. That damned blaggard stabbed me!"

"Were you badly hurt?"

He refocused on her and shook his head. "I don't remember much beyond the agony of the knife's blade ripping into my flesh. If I were to judge by the magnitude of my suffering, the wound was quite substantial." He paused and took a breath. "But I'm afraid the extent of its severity eludes me."

She swallowed. "Ariella must have bound the cut and stopped the bleeding. Do you remember?"

He lightly caressed Bethany's cheek. "I'm sorry, but I don't."

She shuddered in response to the iciness of his fingers and frigid sting of the metal ring he wore. Without thinking, she pushed his hand away. Concern touched his face as he pulled back.

"What's troubling you, my dearest? I'm certain you came to my aid and tended to my wounds. I would never think otherwise, although my recollection *is* murky. It's as though a thick fog has seeped into my brain and nothing is clear."

Bethany nodded. "You're right. Ariella must have patched you up, because you boarded the ship to Annapolis the next day."

"What?" His brows contracted. "That seems improbable. I doubt I could have endured the carriage ride to the wharf."

"But you did." Bethany extended an arm from under the quilts and grabbed the family's history book from the nightstand. "The historical record says you boarded the ship to Annapolis, but were lost at sea." She flipped the pages and pointed to Captain Perry's letter.

"What do you mean by historical records?" His scowl deepened. "May I see that?"

She handed him the book. "The ship's captain wrote that a storm washed you overboard on October 18, 1774."

"I perished? At sea?" He squinted at the page. "No! How can that be? I'm here with you now, in our bedchamber."

She shook her head. "No. You're just a character in my dream. A figment of my imagination. The real Samuel Watts, may he rest in peace, died two hundred and fifty years ago during a storm in the Chesapeake Bay."

Bethany's throat tightened as she watched his face crumple. He turned away, his shoulders heaving. Quiet sobs escaped his throat, growing louder and almost ethereal, until they mimicked the ring tone of her alarm.

Her eyes flew open. Light filled the room, illuminating the history book that lay next to her on the quilt. Her phone was blaring.

Samuel was gone.

Chapter 7: Sailing on the Chesapeake Bay

At the breakfast table, Bethany sipped coffee and tried to focus as she leafed through the Worthington family history book. But her brain, frazzled from last night's interrupted sleep, kept replaying her dream about Samuel and his reaction to the news of his death.

"You look tired, dear," Mrs. Snowden said as she walked into the kitchen. "Didn't you sleep well?"

"Not really. I couldn't stop thinking about Samuel Watts." Which was true, sort of. She didn't want to admit to another dream. "Do you think it's possible he didn't sail to Annapolis that day?"

"Most likely he did. I don't know of any stories that suggest otherwise." Mrs. Snowden sat across from Bethany. "Still, historical records aren't always accurate. Many families fudged the truth to hide the more, shall we say, unsavory aspects of their family lore. Wealthy families, especially. No doubt the Worthingtons would have gone to great lengths to keep secrets." She leaned closer to Bethany. "Why do you ask? Did Ginny have information that says he didn't?"

Bethany shrugged. "No. Just curious." So why was she even considering that something else—like a stab wound—killed him? "Do you know much about Frederick Howard?"

"Only that he was Ariella's second husband." Mrs. Snowden pointed to the history book. "There's probably more information about him in that journal you're reading."

Bethany thumbed through several pages and stopped. "Ariella married Frederick Howard in 1775. Apparently, he was the eldest son of a wealthy landowner in Anne Arundel County."

A wisp of chilly air wafted through the kitchen as Bethany finished the sentence. It left a faint, lingering fragrance—something she'd recently encountered but couldn't quite place. And then she heard a hushed sigh. It was almost inaudible, as though she'd imagined it. But then a grief-filled murmur, barely perceptible, followed.

"Oh god, Ariella. You married him?"

Bethany stood abruptly, rattled by the sound. *Great. Now I'm hearing things.*

Mrs. Snowden looked up, her brow wrinkled with concern. "Are you okay, dear? You look a bit on edge."

"I'm fine. Just groggy. More caffeine will help."

As Bethany refilled her mug from the carafe on the counter, she heard the back door open, then froze as Nick's voice murmured a greeting to Mrs. Snowden. When she turned, he was next to her, reaching for a mug. He searched her face, his smile hesitant.

"Morning, Bethany."

"Nick, I owe you an apology for last night." She whispered, so Mrs. Snowden couldn't eavesdrop. "I shouldn't have taken off so suddenly."

"Did I do something to make you uncomfortable?" He held her gaze, his deep brown eyes friendly, yet cautious. And captivating. She swallowed and took a step back, giving him access to the coffee.

"Yesterday was a long day, and I hadn't fully recovered from traveling." A believable excuse, and much better than admitting she found him gut-wrenchingly appealing, and was afraid of resurrecting desires that belonged in the past.

"That's understandable. A rain check, then?"

"Okay."

His smile broadened into a grin, and it triggered a flush that started in her chest and worked its way upward, heating her cheeks and forehead with a slow burn. Mortified by her reaction to him, Bethany quickly walked back to the table. She needed a distraction, and the history book was the first thing that caught her attention. But something about it was different. She studied the page and realized the paragraph describing Frederick Howard wasn't there. Instead, she saw Ariella and Frederick's wedding announcement.

"That's weird," she mumbled, staring at the text. Had Mrs. Snowden turned the page?

Nick sat next to her. "What's weird?"

"Uh…" Bethany grappled for a believable excuse to explain her surprise. "The announcement for Ariella's marriage to Frederick Howard. She married him eight months after Samuel's disappearance."

"Hmm. It seems like an unusually short mourning period," Mrs. Snowden said.

An image of Samuel, agonizing over the sight of Ariella in Frederick's arms, floated into Bethany's mind. It must have been more than just a friendly embrace if he was ready to stab Frederick. He must have thought something illicit was going on between them.

"Maybe Ariella and Frederick were having an affair." As she blurted out the words, an icy weight, like a hand, touched her shoulder. She stiffened, brushing at the spot to dispel the sensation. But the pressure remained as a puff of cold air skimmed her neck.

"Ariella, why do you mock me?"

The murmur was quiet. But she definitely heard it. The words were more discernible and spoken by a man. She glanced over at Nick.

"Did you say something?"

"No." He sipped his coffee. "But if his wife was having an affair, it would give Samuel a good reason to be angry. And haunt this place."

"Anything's possible, I suppose." Mrs. Snowden stood and started toward the front room. "I'd love to continue the discussion with you two, but guests are checking in today and I need to get ready for their arrival."

Bethany glanced at Nick. Now at a loss for words since they were alone, she focused on the book, fingering one page, then turning to the next while waiting for him to leave. But Nick didn't appear to be in any hurry. He sat at the table, sipping his coffee and studying her, which she confirmed with a sideways glance. Finally, he leaned closer and broke the silence.

"That's some theory. Ariella and Frederick having an affair. How'd you come up with that?"

She looked up, and their eyes met. The depth of his pupils was mesmerizing. Like deep pools. It would be so easy to dive in…

Stop! Breathe. Don't let him get to you. She inhaled, willing herself to resist his gaze, his smile…his…Nickness.

"People are unfaithful all the time."

"I suppose you're right." He maintained his focus on her. "Since you owe me a rain check, how about some Eastern Shore sightseeing this morning? I have the day

56

off."

Bethany tried to ignore his scrutiny, but his deep brown eyes held her captive again, squashing her resolve to distance herself from him.

"The rain check is for a cocktail at that haunted tavern," she said.

"We can add that to the itinerary, but I was thinking we could start with something else."

"What'd you have in mind?"

He grinned. "Sailing. It can be chilly out on the bay, but you should be fine with a few extra layers."

"You're still an avid sailor?"

"It's one of my favorite things. As I recall, you enjoyed it, too."

She hadn't been on a sailboat since her last summer here, and she'd missed it. Her thoughts turned to his wooden dinghy and how the two of them had wedged themselves into its hull, sitting so close that their arms and knees remained in continuous contact. They'd spent hours flitting along the western shoreline of the island, happily enduring waterlogged clothes, chapped lips, and sunburned noses because the strong rush of wind and the sting of salty spray was worth it.

"Your little sailboat *was* fun."

"The *Pipsqueak*." His expression softened. "She was always good for a thrilling ride."

A twinge of melancholy squeezed Bethany's chest as she recalled her last sailing trip with Nick. The sun was bright and the wind perfect as Nick steered the two-person dinghy north toward the Chesapeake Bay Bridge. Once there, he'd told her to hang on as he maneuvered the little craft into a U-turn to head back to Worthington Cove. She'd almost fallen overboard as the boat switched directions, but he grabbed her waist and held her close until they came ashore at Matapeake Beach.

They'd sat on the sand, snatching innocent, hungry kisses while sharing a picnic lunch. The brush of his lips against hers had been exhilarating. She remembered his scent—a combination of warm skin, sunscreen, and salt water—and realized with a pang that he still smelled the same.

She couldn't handle an outing similar to the ones they'd shared back then. Just the two of them, sitting shoulder to shoulder in that tiny boat. Just the thought of it resurrected an old ache that had lain dormant for years.

"Nick, it's been ten years since I've been in a sailboat. Any boat. Honestly, I don't think I can manage a trip in the *Pipsqueak*. As I recall, your sailing skills got us soaked."

He chuckled. "I wouldn't want to take the dinghy out either. I have a larger boat now. A thirty-foot sloop docked at Tilghman's Marina. We could sail her up to the bridge. Maybe even farther north to the tip of the island. Are you game?"

Her gut told her that sailing with Nick was a terrible idea. Although getting out on the bay *was* on her Worthington Cove to-do list. And they wouldn't be sitting knee to knee on a thirty-foot sloop. Besides, it was a sightseeing trip, and nothing more. She'd make sure of that.

"Okay."

"How about I meet you at the marina in an hour? On Dock C. I need to pick up some things before we go out."

"Sure."

"Bring a jacket and sunglasses." He stood and set his mug in the sink. "And don't worry about getting wet.

My sailing abilities have improved immensely over the last ten years."

****

At the edge of the dock, Bethany surveyed the line of sailboats, their bare masts stark against the clear blue sky. Although the sun was bright, a chilly breeze blew in from the bay. She zipped her jacket against the cool air and strolled down the narrow wooden walkway, surveying the boats and speculating on which one belonged to Nick. When she reached the dock's end, she turned back and saw Nick at the opposite end, pulling a large blue cooler. He wore a bright red hoodie with "Maryland" printed across the front.

He stopped midway down the walkway and shouted, "This one's mine." When she reached the stern of the white, single-mast sailboat, he held out his hand to help her climb aboard. *Natalie Rose*, painted in blue script, stretched across the transom. Bethany forced a smile to hide her uneasiness at the other woman's name. She'd assumed Nick was single, so who was Natalie Rose? A former girlfriend? Ex-wife?

"She's not fancy, but quite a step up from the *Pipsqueak*. Come on down and I'll show you around the cabin." He grabbed the cooler and disappeared through a small door just beyond the steering wheel.

Grasping the handrail, she descended four steep, ladder-like steps and took stock of her surroundings. Polished wood paneling glowed in the sunlight streaming through several narrow windows. Built-in sofas lined the left and right walls, and a wooden tabletop stood between them.

Nick pointed to the tiny kitchenette on the right, which included a small oven, two-burner stove, sink, cabinets, and microwave. "This is the galley." He lifted a hinged lid built into the countertop and waved at the space beneath it. "It even has a refrigerator."

Two wooden doors, as tall as the height of the cabin, stood side by side on the left. "What's behind these?" Bethany asked.

His eyes were playful as he opened one and motioned her forward. "This is the aft stateroom. The main sleeping quarters." She leaned in and saw a full-size mattress covered with a navy-blue quilt and throw pillows that matched the ones on the sofas. Above the bed, light poured through a narrow window.

The other door concealed a tiny bathroom with a toilet and sink. "This is the head."

They continued forward to a paneled wall and another door at the bow. Behind it, a V-shaped platform formed another sleeping area.

"This is the forward berth."

Bethany ran her hand over the navy-blue bedspread. Whoever decorated his boat's interior had done a wonderful job, and her chest constricted, wondering if it was Natalie Rose.

"It's beautiful. Even though I loved your little boat, I can see why you upgraded. It's very cozy. You could live here if you wanted."

"I don't know about living aboard, but she's perfect for overnight trips. I've only done a couple, though. Mainly, I stick to day sails."

"Where exactly are we going today?" she asked, directing her thoughts toward something other than Nick's overnight sailing trips and who went with him.

"To Love Point on the northern tip of Kent Island." He pointed to the cooler. "I brought lunch. On our way back, we can anchor near Matapeake Beach and eat on the boat."

"Oh." Her breath hitched when he mentioned their lunch destination. Did he remember their last outing there?

Before she could say anything else, he grabbed the ladder's handrails, quickly climbed up to the cockpit, and called down from the deck. "I'll check the lines and get the mainsail and jib ready for hoisting. We'll wait and put up the sails once we're out in the bay."

She carefully followed him. "What can I do to help?"

"Nothing right now."

Bethany perched on a cushion-covered bench/storage locker at the stern and watched as he checked the sails and ropes. He handled the tasks with grace and confidence, and she felt a tug of disappointment knowing he'd moved on without her, mastering this boat and sailing it with someone else.

He started the engine. "Ready?"

She nodded, inhaling the water's briny scent. Intermittent screeches from seagulls floating above accompanied the low drone of the engine. As Nick guided the boat out to the bay, they passed an assortment of large and small sailboats, fishing boats, and power cruisers tied up at the other docks. Once he cleared the marina's jetties, Nick cut the engine and faced her.

"You're my crew today. Can I put you in charge of the helm while I hoist the mainsail?"

"Me?" She stared at him, doubting her ability to carry out his request. "What do I need to do?"

"Just make sure the bow points directly into the wind. I'll show you." He pointed to a gauge built into the cockpit's center console. "This needle shows the wind direction. Hold her steady so it hovers near the marking at the top."

She studied the instrument panel. "This boat is much more complicated than the dinghy. Are you sure I can handle it?"

His lips curved into his crooked grin. "Absolutely."

As Bethany gripped the wheel, Nick let out the rope to his right to lift the mainsail, then secured it. He'd handled the sail with ease, and she imagined his muscles flexing underneath his sweatshirt. He'd always been fit and toned as a teenager, but now he radiated power. And it was intoxicating.

"I'll unfurl the jib sail next, and then we'll be all set." He readjusted some settings on the console and the boat started to glide through the water. Then he let out the rope on his left and the second sail opened. Almost immediately, the boat picked up speed as the wind propelled it toward the Bay Bridge.

Once Nick took over the helm, Bethany returned to her seat and leaned into the breeze. She'd missed this—the warm sun, fluttering sails, salty air whipping her skin, and the steady thump of waves smacking the side of the hull. All the tension she'd been hoarding drained away, left behind in the wake as the boat pushed forward.

Nick made a few more adjustments to the instruments, then sat next to her, using the railing as a backrest while resting his fingers on the wheel. He lifted his face toward the sun, and she scrutinized him with a side look, her ogling masked by sunglasses while she took in his wind-tousled hair, rosy cheeks, and chapped lips. He appeared serene as he harnessed the power of the wind to control the boat.

"It's peaceful out here," she said. "I can see why you enjoy sailing so much."

"My mom always told me I had saltwater instead of blood running through my veins." He chuckled. "She's probably right."

"I believe it. There's something addictive about the water. I can feel its pull. Like a siren song."

His expression turned thoughtful as he focused on the bay. "We have that in common. We always did, even when we were teens. The water connects us."

She'd believed that, too, a long time ago. But his unexplained silence, her broken heart, and new relationships for each of them—Natalie Rose for him and Owen for her—had severed that connection.

Nick put a hand on her shoulder, his voice breaking into her thoughts. "Look. Over there. Off the starboard side. Canada geese."

A flock of water birds flew overhead, interrupting the quiet with their loud, squawking honks.

"They're beautiful." She watched as they approached, lowering their legs and then skidding along the water's surface to make a graceful landing by the tall grasses near the shore.

"We're getting near Matapeake Beach. Mind if I share a fun fact?"

"Please do. Sightseeing tours always come with a knowledgeable tour guide, right?"

"Yep. Just think of me as Nick Dorsey, private guide extraordinaire." He grinned. "Believe it or not, ferries ran from Matapeake to Annapolis in the early nineteen hundreds. See the clubhouse back there? It was the ferry terminal building back then and served food and drinks to people waiting to board."

The narrow stretch of beige sand came into view just beyond the clump of marsh grass and shoreline trees. A couple sat at the water's edge, laughing as a small dog gingerly stepped into the surf and backed up as the waves washed over its paws.

Her heart thudded. "I remember this place. We sailed here in the dinghy and sat on the beach." *And we hung onto each other as though our lives depended on it. Neither of us wanted to let go, and I thought we'd be together forever.*

"Yeah. We gave the *Pipsqueak* quite a workout that summer, didn't we?" He faced her, his sunglasses rendering his expression unreadable. "And I loved every minute. That was the best summer I've ever had."

His words pricked at her chest, threatening to open the wound that had taken much too long to heal. That summer had been the best for her, too. So what happened? Why didn't he stay in touch? This was the perfect opportunity to ask him, but the question died on her lips. It was better if she didn't know.

Nick pointed out more features along the shoreline as they sailed past Matapeake Beach. Both were quiet as the wind pushed the *Natalie Rose* closer to the massive concrete piers supporting the Bay Bridge. Bethany spied a couple of boats ahead of them, and others passing by, heading south. To the west, silhouettes of several oil tankers were visible in the distance.

"You up for another fun fact?" he asked as the bridge loomed ahead of them.

"Sure."

He smiled. "The Chesapeake Bay Bridge is formally named the Governor William Preston Lane, Junior Memorial Bridge because Governor Lane initiated its construction in the late nineteen forties. The first span was built in the early nineteen fifties and the second in the nineteen seventies. Both spans are just over four miles long."

"Impressive. And you know this because…?"

"I like the bridge, and I like to know random facts about Kent Island. After all, it's the biggest island in the Chesapeake Bay with almost thirty-two square miles of land."

"I see that nerdy kid from years ago still lives inside of you."

"Some things never change." He laughed and grasped the wheel, guiding the boat underneath the bridge's steel girders. Overhead, a line of cars snaked along its eastbound span. Bethany marveled at his ability to navigate the thirty-foot boat. He handled it with certainty, as though he'd been sailing the *Natalie Rose* his entire life.

"How long have you had this boat?" she asked, working up the courage to ask him about its namesake.

"About five years now. She's a used boat, almost twenty years old, but handles well. Much easier than the dinghy, believe it or not."

With her fingers curled into anxious fists, Bethany tried to sound nonchalant as she tossed out her next question. "I'm curious. Who is she named after?"

"My older sister."

"You have a sister?" *Natalie Rose isn't his girlfriend!* Although she didn't recall ever meeting his sister, relief lightened her mood. "I didn't know."

He hesitated for a moment, as if weighing his answer. When he replied, his voice held a trace of sadness. "She had health issues and wasn't around much."

"Oh." Bethany paused, trying to think of what to say. Although interested in knowing more about his sister, she didn't want to pry. "Well, I bet Natalie is thrilled that you named your boat after her. It's a beautiful name."

A slight smile tugged at his lips. "I'm glad you think so."

Neither said much as they sailed farther north. Bethany savored the experience of gliding through the water while Nick focused on the helm. Mesmerized by the rush of the wind and the taste of salt on her lips, she lost track of time and started when he broke the silence.

"Love Point is just ahead on the starboard side. Steamboats and ferries used to dock there in the early nineteen hundreds. There's a story behind the name that dates back to the sixteen hundreds."

"Okay. Let's hear it, Mr. Tour Guide."

"According to local legend, two lovers were washed ashore there in an embrace. Apparently, their love was forbidden, and they preferred to die together rather than live apart."

"That's so sad."

"Love Point also had a Chessie sighting."

"A what?"

"The Chesapeake Bay has its own sea monster named Chessie. People have been reporting sightings since the nineteen thirties. Around thirty years ago, a man and woman saw Chessie out in the bay near Love Point. Caught it on video, too."

"That's pretty amazing. And a bit unbelievable."

"Maybe. But Chessie was sighted again about three years ago. West of here in the Magothy River. Witnesses said she was about twenty-five feet long. Didn't get pictures, though. Apparently, Chessie is very shy."

"Sounds like it. Which makes it hard to believe something like that exists."

"Yeah. A lot of things around here are hard to believe in. But that doesn't mean they're not real."

"Like ghosts, I suppose."

"Exactly."

He grinned, and she pictured his dark eyes crinkled into slits behind his sunglasses. A moment later, he switched his focus to the instrument panel.

"We're at the tip of the island. It's time to change course and head back. Ready to tack?"

"Sure. But I don't remember what that means."

"Since we're turning around, I need you to help pull the sail to the other side." He pointed to a rope. "Grab the end of that rope. When I say *hard-a-lee*, unwind it completely off the winch." He motioned toward a second rope. "Then use the winch handle to tighten that other rope."

Bethany grabbed the first rope, fidgeting with nervous energy.

"Ready?" he asked.

She gulped. "Yes."

"Hard-a-lee."

She unwound one rope and quickly tightened the other as the mainsail swung from one side of the mast to the other. The boat shifted, leaning to the left while the bow made a wide arc across the bay. She clutched the lifeline as Nick scanned the water and peered at the instrument panel while turning the steering wheel. He looked over and smiled when he caught her studying him.

"See, a successful tack and neither of us got soaked."

"It's a lot different from the *Pipsqueak*."

"Sailing that little boat is exciting, and I still take her out once in a while. But more often I prefer a calmer, more reflective sail on the *Natalie Rose*." He shrugged, and a chuckle escaped his lips. "Maybe I'm getting too old for the exhilaration of sailing a dinghy."

"I don't believe that for a minute." Bethany laughed and reclaimed her spot next to him. "But I understand why you like this boat."

"Hopefully you like it, too."

She did. Sailing a boat like the *Natalie Rose* was the perfect way to spend time on the water. She'd miss this when back in Oklahoma City and her breath faltered at the thought of going home.

"I do. It's nice."

Nick flashed her a grin, then pointed to the approaching Bay Bridge. "After the bridge, we'll be at our next destination in about fifteen minutes."

****

Nick joined Bethany in the cockpit after lowering the sails and dropping anchor. The *Natalie Rose,* bobbing gently, provided them with a clear view of Matapeake Beach. Aside from the couple with the little dog and several seabirds wading in the waves, the narrow stretch of beach was empty.

"Are you hungry?"

"It depends. What'd you pack for lunch?"

"Coffee, for one thing. Want some?"

"Yes, please." Although the sun was bright, the air seemed colder where they'd anchored. She'd worn a T-shirt and sweater under her jacket, but it wasn't enough to keep her from shivering.

"Wait here." He disappeared through the entryway and came back carrying an insulated carafe and two mugs. To Bethany's dismay, her body shook as he poured the steaming coffee. He stopped to scrutinize her, then scooped up the mugs.

"I can tell you're cold. Let's eat in the cabin. It's warmer down there."

She followed him down the ladder and settled into the cushioned sofa. Nick handed her the filled mug, and she took a sip.

"Better?" he asked.

"Definitely."

"I stopped at Lindy's on my way to the marina and picked up a couple of shrimp salad hoagies." He rummaged in the cooler, pulled out two paper-wrapped bundles, and set them on the table. "It's one of their specialties, along with crab cakes."

"Thank you. You're being so nice. Especially after—"

Nick faced her, his brows raised as he leaned in. "After what?"

His proximity left her lightheaded, and she scooted away. For her own well-being, she had to resist his charm. "After I left you standing in the street last night. I still feel bad about that."

"Don't worry about it." He opened a nearby cabinet and retrieved paper plates, napkins, and plastic utensils.

"I was exhausted," she continued. "I haven't slept well the last couple of nights."

"That's not surprising." He stopped and caught her gaze, his mouth forming an impish grin. "Since you're staying in a haunted house and contenting with ghosts."

He reached into the cooler again and retrieved a bag of potato chips, two bottles of lemon/lime seltzer water, and a white deli-style container. "Lindy's makes good coleslaw, too."

Ignoring his ghost jab, she eyed the lunch he laid out in front of her. She hadn't expected him to bring a meal, much less an impressive spread from Lindy's. "You thought of everything,"

"I aim to please, ma'am."

She laughed as she unwrapped a sandwich and put it on a plate, along with a generous serving of coleslaw.

"You're spoiling me with all this Maryland seafood. I can't remember the last time I had shrimp salad." She bit into the roll and savored the firm texture of the shrimp, the crunch of celery, and the tang of crab seasoning and mayonnaise. "Oh, this is amazing."

"Consider it your birthright. After all, you have roots here on Kent Island." He bit into his sandwich and studied her. "Not just your parents, but also your look-alike—Miss Worthington. You can't deny the resemblance."

"I'm related to her on my mom's side."

"Are you a descendant of Samuel Watts, too?"

"That's what my Aunt Ginny says." Determined not to blurt out information about last night's dream with Samuel or the eerie experiences in the kitchen this morning, she took another bite of her sandwich and surveyed their surroundings, looking for a diversion.

"This boat is like a floating RV. Do you take many overnight trips?"

"Not as many as I'd like." He grabbed a handful of chips and dumped them on his plate. "I know you're trying to distract me and change the subject. Why don't you want to talk about Samuel? Did something happen?"

She shrugged. "Nothing worth mentioning."

His brows shot up and he gave her a knowing smirk. "His ghost visited you in a dream again last night, didn't it?"

She scooped a forkful of coleslaw, avoiding his gaze. Why did he have to be so perceptive? "I don't believe in ghosts, remember?"

"Believing isn't such a crazy thing," he replied. "And you've had enough encounters to at least *consider* the possibility that his spirit is reaching out to you."

"They're just dreams, Nick." She slid the coleslaw into her mouth. "And you're right," she continued, pointing at her plate. "This coleslaw is good."

"I never tell tales when it comes to food. Or ghosts." He bit into his sandwich. "I bet you felt Samuel's presence in the kitchen today, too. When you encountered something *weird*. I could tell by your expression."

"Is that so?"

"It is. And I have a proposal for you."

She watched as he lifted a takeout box from the cooler and popped off the lid. Nestled inside was a huge slice of white cake with a thick, creamy filling. Bethany could smell its rich, citrusy aroma.

"Lindy's lemon cake," he announced proudly, displaying it as though he were holding a jeweled crown. "It's the best on the Eastern Shore. They only had one slice left, so I snagged it. But I might consider sharing."

"I never turn down cake, even if it's only half a slice."

He flaunted the cake in front of her. "Here's the deal. I'll split this slice with you. But only if you tell me all about your dream with Samuel last night and what you experienced in the kitchen this morning."

She considered him and the cake. Should she tell him about the dream? Probably not. Sharing what had occurred this morning was out of the question. More than likely, the voice-like sounds and cold spots were merely quirks of an old house and not related to Samuel's spirit. And if she ever believed otherwise—which was *highly* improbable—she wouldn't talk about it with Nick. It was better to stick with irrefutable facts.

"No, thanks."

"What?" His mouth twitched and his eyes reflected amusement. "I thought you never turned down cake."

"I don't." She'd teach him to tease her with sweets. With a laugh, she grabbed the box from his hands and held it out of his reach. "If you want intel on Samuel, it'll cost you the entire slice."

He flashed her a grin and eyed the cake. "You drive a hard bargain, but I accept."

She lifted a generous bite of the dessert into her mouth. "Mm, this cake is worth every penny you paid."

"I'm holding up my end of the deal." He propped his elbows on the table, his knuckles supporting his chin as he watched her. "Now it's your turn. Spill it."

Between bites, she recapped what she'd learned about Samuel from Aunt Ginny.

"That's it? You sound like you're quoting facts from a history book." Nick leaned in until his face was mere inches away from hers.

"That's what I know," she said, loading the last bite of cake on her fork.

Without warning, he grabbed her hand, steered the fork toward his mouth, and ate the last bite. He closed his eyes and sighed loudly. "You're right. This cake is amazing!"

"Hey! Don't think you'll get any more information out of me."

"That's okay. The cake was worth it." With his hand still around hers, Nick held her gaze. "Besides, I'm sure you'll be a believer soon enough. The stories about a ghost in Horatio House have been around for as long as I can remember, and I'm convinced they're true."

"Oh, really? What makes you so sure about that?"

"Because I have a story of my own."

She raised her brows. "Tell me."

Snorting with amusement, he shook his head. "When you're ready to share yours, I'll share mine."

Their eyes locked for a long moment, and his grin morphed into something melancholy. The expression was familiar, yet hard to define. Was it longing? Regret? Or was she projecting her own emotions—desire and confusion—that had resurfaced after all these years? She averted her gaze.

"We should head back to the marina." He stood abruptly, stowed their trash in the empty cooler, and then clambered up the ladder. When Bethany emerged from the cabin, he was already at the bow of the boat, preparing to hoist the sails.

"Crew reporting for duty, Captain," she called out from the cockpit.

He looked up, his easy smile erasing the awkwardness she'd felt. "We'll hoist the mainsail first, then the jib."

"Got it." She positioned herself at the helm and watched the wind gauge while he lifted the sails and secured the ropes. As the *Natalie Rose* picked up speed, he joined her at the stern.

The sea air caressed their faces as they sat side by side. Time passed quickly, and Bethany wasn't ready for the trip to end when he moved to the bow of the boat and lowered the sails. She wanted to continue southward, sitting next to Nick and absorbing the magic of the bay. Something about him pulled her in. Just like it had ten years ago.

When he returned to the cockpit and revved the engine, an ache settled in her chest at the signal their outing was coming to an end. Moments later, he expertly steered the *Natalie Rose* through the marina and into her slip.

"That was fun." Bethany picked up her bag. "Thanks for taking me out."

She walked toward the transom and was about to hop onto the dock when Nick placed his hand on her arm.

"I'm glad you came today." He studied her, his dark eyes wistful, as though he, too, was reluctant to wrap up the outing. "I've missed this. Sailing together. Spending time with you. Maybe we can go again while you're here."

His touch sent a rush of heat racing through her body, and she knew their shared appreciation of the bay wasn't the cause of the spark. She breathed deeply to dispel the fire in her cheeks, and inhaled his warm, salty scent. Yearning stabbed at her gut, and she looked away, wishing her body didn't crave more than a casual touch from him.

Oh, lord, don't let me fall for him again.

"We'll see," she replied, quickly jumping off the boat and out of his reach, determined not to let her guard down. She couldn't handle another heartbreak.

Chapter 8: It's All About History

Instead of taking the direct route back to Horatio House, Bethany walked north to Main Street and the Toasted Bean. Strolling through the center of town was a perfect way to clear her head of Nick Dorsey. She loved the historic ambiance of the boxy, colonial-style houses with wooden shutters and wide verandas, a reminder of her direct connection to the town. That her parents had swapped the simple beauty of Worthington Cove for the congested bustle of Oklahoma City had always left her mystified. Their roots and family were here.

At the coffee bar, Bethany ordered a mocha latte and grabbed a turkey sandwich for dinner. Still basking in the glow from being out on the bay and reluctant to call it a day, she paused at the town library on her way back to the inn, then bounded up the concrete steps and went inside, hoping her aunt was still there.

The library's front desk was deserted, so she called out softly. Almost immediately, Aunt Ginny emerged from the adjacent room, her eyes warm and welcoming.

"Bethany! I was going to call you tonight." She walked over to the desk and retrieved a worn leather-bound book. "I found more information about Samuel Watts that might answer why he was sailing to Annapolis the day he fell overboard."

She set the volume on the counter and studied Bethany, grinning. "You're positively radiant. Your date

75

last night with Nick must have gone well. I've been wondering about it all morning."

Bethany gulped one last mouthful of coffee and tossed the empty latte cup in the trash can. "It wasn't a date, Aunt Ginny. Just dinner. The crab cakes were amazing, by the way. And this morning we went sailing on the bay."

"Oh? Sounds like you two are rekindling old feelings."

"We're just friends. And today's trip was a sightseeing tour. That's all."

"I see." Aunt Ginny peered at Bethany over her glasses. "Well, whatever it was, I'm glad you're getting out instead of hiding away at the inn and moping over Owen. And, for the record, I still think Nick deserves a second chance. Seeing him again seems to agree with you."

Aunt Ginny had a point. Nick *did* deserve another chance, but just as a friend. While reluctant to admit it, Bethany realized the connection between her and Nick had somehow persevered. Spending time with him was enjoyable and it might help speed up the process of getting over Owen and moving on. But she wouldn't become attached to Nick. She wasn't up for any more romance-related anguish.

Bethany caught Aunt Ginny staring at her, as though waiting for a full-blown recap. Time to change the subject. She pointed to the slim book on the counter.

"So, you mentioned you found more information on Samuel?"

"Oh! Yes. The day after Samuel disappeared at sea, there was a meeting in Annapolis to discuss the fate of a local merchant who smuggled British tea aboard his ship.

The community considered his crime to be quite serious. I bet Samuel planned to be there, and that's why he was sailing across the Chesapeake."

"Thanks, Aunt Ginny." That lined up with Samuel's comments in her dream. He and Frederick were traveling to a meeting.

"Happy to help. I was doing more research anyway for the history festival. Which reminds me. I have a huge favor to ask." Aunt Ginny retrieved a packet from her desk and handed it to Bethany. "The festival committee is meeting this coming Tuesday. Since you've handled big fundraising affairs for your organization, I was hoping you'd give us some pointers on recruiting sponsors. This is what we have so far."

"Is this a new event?"

Aunt Ginny nodded. "It's part of the mayor's plan to promote Worthington Cove as a tourist destination. Like Chestertown does with its annual reenactment of the 1774 British tea protest. We're excited about it, but once we started planning, we realized it's too much for a volunteer committee to take on. So we've petitioned the town council to hire a festival manager. In the meantime, I'd really appreciate any advice you can offer to get us headed in the right direction."

Bethany thumbed through the pages in the folder, noting the project's scope and limited time window. No wonder they wanted help. The magnitude of what they envisioned was challenging for an experienced committee. For a newly formed group of volunteers, it would be overwhelming.

"I'm happy to read through it and make notes. But this date is less than a year away. That's not a lot of time to pull everything together, especially when starting from scratch."

Her aunt's shoulders drooped. "I'm not convinced the town council realizes how much time and resources are required to pull off a successful festival. But it has the potential to give the town's businesses a much-needed boost. And it could be the start of an annual Worthington Cove tradition."

"To make it workable, they'll need to hire someone fairly soon. A person who has experience in event planning."

"You're right. And I know it really isn't fair for me to ask this, but while we're waiting for their decision on a manager, could you give us a list of what needs to be done to get started?"

"Of course." Bethany gathered her things. "I'll get something back to you soon, maybe even tomorrow."

Aunt Ginny brightened as she embraced Bethany. "You're a lifesaver. Thank you." She released Bethany, stepped toward her desk, then stopped. "I almost forgot. Would you like to have dinner at my house tomorrow night? Around six?"

"I'd love to. Can I bring anything?"

Aunt Ginny touched the book in Bethany's hand. "Just bring this back. It really shouldn't leave the library, but I trust you to take care of it. And as far as dinner goes, it will only be the two of us, and I've got everything covered."

****

That night, Bethany settled into her bed and examined the book from the town library. Aunt Ginny had marked a page explaining the politics that caused the Maryland colonists' anger over the British tea. After reading a few paragraphs, Bethany's eyelids drooped.

She attempted to continue, but the sunny afternoon on the bay had drained her energy. Instead of struggling to stay alert, she burrowed under the quilts, hoping to get a good night's sleep without dreaming of Samuel Watts.

"The meeting. I'm certain I didn't go." Samuel's voice.

Not again. "What meeting?" Groggy from sleep, she forced her eyes open and found him hovering over her with the history book in his hand. She recoiled, sucking in cold air and his lavender scent.

"The meeting in Annapolis regarding the British tea smuggler. The one Howard asked me to attend." Samuel sighed impatiently, as though she should know this.

"I know you didn't go to the meeting. We've been through this." Exhaling, she turned away. "You sailed to Annapolis and fell overboard on the way there. Please let me go back to sleep."

"That's not what I meant. I'm sure I never set foot on that ship the next morning, and I most certainly did not fall off it." He clutched her forearm, holding on so tightly that she felt the chill of his fingertips through the quilt.

Irritated by the force of his grasp, Bethany yanked her arm away and threw back the quilts. She'd had enough of him interrupting her sleep and was determined to end these dreams once and for all. Inhaling deeply, she got out of bed and confronted him.

"You're wrong, and I need some sleep. Please go."

His features registered shock as he stared back. "Ariella, why are you asking me to take my leave? Have you lost your compassion for me?"

She glared at him with frustration. "Look at me. I'm not Ariella."

His lips pursed in defiance as he stared at her. "What? Of course you are."

"Listen carefully. I'm Bethany, Ariella's descendant. She was my great-great-great-great-great grandmother. She died over two hundred years ago…and so did you."

A frown creased his forehead as he hovered closer to scan her face. She stared back, determined that he see and accept the truth. After silently scrutinizing her for what seemed like an eternity, he replied.

"The cute round freckle is missing from your cheek. Plus, I do not detect the tiny scar that marked your lip after we tumbled into the creek." A single tear slid down his cheek. "Although the resemblance is remarkable, I can see that you're not my Ariella. Your countenance is different, too. There's a brusqueness about you, which she didn't possess." He continued staring, and then his eyes flickered with comprehension.

"Miss Bethany, if you are her descendant, does that mean…"

She released a heavy sigh in response. "You're my great-great-great-great-great-grandfather."

Samuel peered down at her, his smile soft. "I have a granddaughter?"

"Yes, you do. About five generations of them. And this one is very tired. So now that you're clear on who I am, would you please stop bothering me? I really need my rest, and dreaming about you is exhausting."

"Wait. You think you're dreaming?" He extended his hand and pressed it to her cheek. "That's completely inaccurate, dearest granddaughter. Because I'm as real as you are."

Bethany flinched at the iciness of his fingers and the

cold bite of his ring. No, he was a creation of her imagination, nothing more. But maybe playing along with his conviction would get him out of her head once and for all. It was worth a shot.

"Okay then. I'll try to help, but I won't guarantee this will work. And you have to leave me alone after this." She backed out of his reach and held his gaze until he dipped his chin in agreement. "Why don't you start by telling me what else you remember?"

Inhaling deeply, Samuel grasped Bethany's hand and concentrated on her face. "I was reviewing the plantation's receipts in my study. It was very late when I went to our bedroom to retire for the night. But the bed was empty, so I went downstairs to look for you…uh, Ariella."

"And you found her in the salon?"

He nodded, his attention straying from her as he focused, unseeing, beyond her head. "I never trusted Howard. I knew he loved her, that he was the first to capture her heart and propose marriage. But her father rejected the match because Howard's family was Roman Catholic and the Worthingtons were Protestant."

"And then what happened?"

The air grew colder as Samuel continued. "When I reached the main foyer, I overheard Ariella and Howard talking. He was professing his love for her, begging her to leave me and start a new life with him. And…he spoke about our first-born son, Malcolm."

"Oh?" The comment piqued her curiosity. "What'd he say?"

Samuel's fingers tightened into fists as his brow drew into a scowl. "Howard spoke as if Malcolm was *his* son. He urged Ariella to tell me the boy wasn't my child,

81

that Malcolm was his bastard." Samuel paused, his mouth contorting into a grimace.

"Ariella said no, she wouldn't do that. She told him there was no proof. That I was her husband, and she loved me, and she regarded him as a past acquaintance and nothing more." Samuel refocused on Bethany, his eyes moist. "But she didn't deny the possibility that Howard was the boy's father."

As he spoke, her thoughts turned toward Owen, and her chest tightened at the memory of his indiscretion. "I'm so sorry, Samuel." She swiped at her cheeks. "I know how much it hurts when you discover the person you love and trust is keeping a secret." *It's like they've plunged a searing blade into your heart.*

His lips pressed into a hard line. "I loved her more than anything. But I never allowed myself to believe she felt the same."

"But you heard Ariella tell Frederick she loved you. Why would you doubt her?"

"Because her father arranged our marriage. She never protested, always presented herself as a loving wife who adored me. In return, I did everything in my power to be worthy of her love and respect. Even so, I knew I wasn't her choice, that her heart belonged to another."

He sighed. "When Howard claimed my son as his own, I became angry. And then, when I saw him embrace my wife, I completely lost my temper, even though she pushed him away. I rushed over to Howard with all rational thought cast aside, as though a ferocious beast had possessed me. I must have been holding my hunting knife, because I—" Samuel stopped and closed his eyes.

Bethany watched his face crumple, completely

understanding his desire to lash out after hearing such news. When she'd found the unfamiliar red corset under Owen's bed, she wanted to rip it—and the woman who owned it—to shreds.

"Samuel, what did you do?"

He opened his eyes and blinked, as though surprised by his surroundings, then sat on the mattress. His shoulders sagged as Bethany settled next to him.

"I attacked him and we fought. Then—" Samuel paused, unfocused, as though he were summoning a replay of the event, before he fixed his gaze back on her. "Ariella screamed. She couldn't have known what we would do. That we'd try to destroy each other. I felt the blade rip my chest and knew the sticky wetness on my skin was my blood. I heard her sobbing as pain overtook me."

He stared at the wall, his lips forming unsaid words before he spoke. "I remember lying on the floor, attempting to move my arms and legs, but my body wouldn't respond. I was too tired. Then someone grabbed my feet and dragged me."

Bethany remained silent as she watched him work his way through the memory. She wanted him to uncover whatever he was searching for—the thing her subconscious must be trying to recollect through him. Maybe it was a long-forgotten anecdote or some tidbit she'd read. And now her sleeping mind was using Samuel to reconcile that information with historical records. Why else would these images keep invading her sleep? Her own mind couldn't fabricate something so devastating, could it?

To end these dreams once and for all, Bethany needed to speed things up. She reached over and touched

Samuel's hand. "Ariella must have moved you to make you more comfortable and dress your wounds so you could travel the next day."

"No." He refocused on her, shaking his head. "An endless amount of time seemed to pass before sharp edges scraped against my shoulders and the back of my head started bumping against hard stone, as though I was sliding down a set of stairs." He shut his eyes, his forehead again furrowing. "When the movement stopped, I felt dirt against my palms. The air was cool and smelled of damp earth, like I was lying in a cave. I found the strength to look around, and I saw shelves against a stone wall. And then the sound began, resonating over and over in my ears. I couldn't place it at first." He hesitated, as though reliving the moment in his head. "Then I realized what I was hearing."

Bethany grasped his icy fingers, ignoring the cold sting from the ring he wore, and pushed him to continue. "What was it?"

"The faint crunch of metal against hardened soil, followed by the soft patter of falling dirt. Someone was digging."

Samuel opened his eyes, staring wildly at Bethany as he grasped at the sides of his head and emitted a low, agonized moan. It penetrated her skull and settled behind her forehead as an intense throbbing ache.

"Oh, my god, Samuel." Desperate for relief, she rubbed the skin just above her eyebrows. "That sound you're making. Please stop it! It's giving me a headache."

The moan ceased immediately. She glanced at him, startled at the sadness and despair radiating from his face. Grief clutched at her heart. Whatever he remembered must have been shattering. When Samuel spoke again, bewilderment filled his voice. "How could she let Howard do this?"

Do what? Did she even want to know? Convinced she couldn't handle any more of his agony, Bethany willed herself to wake up. Instead, an uninvited question escaped her lips. "What did he do?"

The room's temperature plummeted, and Bethany's breath turned to fog. Samuel looked beyond her at some impalpable horror and whispered, as if to himself, "He was digging my grave."

She stared at him, stunned by his words. "No. That couldn't have happened. The ship's captain wrote to Ariella. You were washed overboard in the Chesapeake Bay."

His lower lip quivered as he shook his head. "I never boarded that ship. I managed one last glimpse of my surroundings as someone dragged me across the floor, and I realized Howard was pulling me into a hole he had dug in the root cellar. As I lay there, with no strength to resist, dirt rained down on my face, pummeling my eyelids and blocking my nose until I could no longer breathe."

He paused and refocused on her, his eyes questioning. "Why did she let this happen?" He swiped at a tear. "I'm her husband. The father of her children. Yet she let Howard murder me."

Chapter 9: Foul Play in the Root Cellar?

Samuel's murder allegation was like a heavy stone weighing her down. How could she dream up such a terrible fate for him when the historical records depicted a different story?

"What's the matter, dear?"

Bethany looked up, her coffee untouched, to see Mrs. Snowden peering at her.

"Does Horatio House have a root cellar?"

Mrs. Snowden leaned in, brimming with interest. "That's quite an unusual question. I don't know, but we can find out. Is there a particular reason you want to know?"

"The historical records all say that Samuel's body was never recovered. What if he never left the house? What if…" Did she dare spit out the words? The notion that Frederick murdered Samuel was far-fetched. That she even considered the possibility was insane.

Mrs. Snowden's eyes grew wide. "You dreamed about him again, didn't you?"

Bethany considered her response. A truthful answer would, without a doubt, prompt a demand for full disclosure of her latest dream. Plus, it would set off Mrs. Snowden's chatter about ghosts and spirits. And, of course, she would tell Nick. And then Bethany would have to deal with his "you're being haunted" banter. But then again, if she talked it out, maybe she could come to terms with whatever was nagging her about Samuel's story and stop dreaming about him. Was it worth it?

Exhaling, she braced herself and took the plunge. "I don't know what's with me. My sleeping brain conjures up ideas that are just…outrageous."

"Now you have to tell me."

"What if Frederick Howard stabbed Samuel and disposed of his body?" She gulped her now-lukewarm coffee and waited for Mrs. Snowden's haunted house spiel.

"In the root cellar?" The innkeeper nodded, understanding reflected in her face. "You think he's down there." As she spoke, the back door swung open and Nick sauntered into the kitchen.

"Who's down where? Are you two talking about me?" He grinned at Bethany as he sauntered to the coffeemaker.

Her cheeks flushed as Mrs. Snowden relayed the details of their conversation and asked him about the root cellar. She hadn't expected Nick to find out about her dream so quickly. Why was he here, anyway? It was Saturday. He glanced at Bethany as he listened to his aunt. Immediately, the heat in her skin, plus the pesky tingle that seemed to erupt in her gut whenever he was around, intensified.

"When I was a kid, we played in an underground room by the stream," he said. "Could that be a root cellar? There wasn't anything in there besides some old wooden shelves mounted on stone walls. We converted it into our secret fort and furnished it with odds and ends we collected. It was a great summer hangout. Nice and cool."

"Think you can still get there?" Mrs. Snowden

asked.

"Maybe. We used landmarks to guide us, but I haven't tried to find it in years." He turned to Bethany, his eyes playful, as he poured coffee. "Shall we look for it now?"

"What? No!"

The words came out before she could stop them. Hunting for the two hundred-and-fifty-year-old burial site of a murder victim was a terrible idea. Particularly when said murder was merely speculation based on a dream. Even if they found the root cellar, what would that prove? Nothing. And spending time there with Nick could be extremely awkward.

Bethany conjured her best apologetic smile. "It's just that I don't want to waste your time. Like you said, there really isn't anything down there."

"It wouldn't be a waste at all. There's no better way to spend a Saturday morning than exploring. Besides, I'm curious to see if I can still find it."

Uh-oh. Not good. Didn't he get the hint? "I'm sure you have other, more pressing things to do."

As she spoke, the temperature in the room dipped. She rubbed her arms against the chill.

"Nope, nothing planned that outranks a hike in the woods." He paused, puzzled. "Are you cold?"

She shook her head. "No. Just felt a draft."

"It's probably the wind blowing through gaps around the window casings. They haven't been caulked in a while." He raised his brows and smirked. "Or maybe you felt a ghost."

Great, the ghost talk again. She sighed. At least he'd stopped pushing the root cellar search. "I'm going to ignore your ghost comment, since this house is more likely to be drafty than haunted. But—"

"Miss Bethany, you must find me and reveal Howard as the murderer he is. To make things right."

She frowned. That wasn't a groaning floor beam or a wheezing radiator. The words were distinct, and the voice was male. Yet she was certain Nick hadn't spoken. Whatever had caused her dreams was now interfering with her waking mind. Probably her lack of sleep.

"But?" Nick's voice.

She had to convince her subconscious brain that Samuel's remains weren't down there. Which meant accepting Nick's offer to search for the root cellar. They'd find it, take a look, see nothing, and leave. End of story.

"Since you're all set for an outing, I'll tag along. Mainly to confirm there's nothing in the root cellar. Let me get my sweater, and I'll meet you in the kitchen."

"Sounds good." He shot her a grin. "As soon as I down some coffee and pack a few things, I'll be ready to go."

****

Half an hour later, Bethany followed Nick to the edge of a small thicket behind Horatio House. He paused next to an oak tree that grew on the perimeter of the wooded area and adjusted the backpack strapped over his shoulders. The air was chilly despite the bright midmorning sun, and quite a few orange and red leaves still clung to branches.

"So you think Samuel was murdered and dumped in the root cellar?" He flashed his familiar crooked smile at her.

"It was just a dream. There's nothing down there, and we're about to prove it."

He shrugged, his eyes reflecting amusement as they moved along the stand of trees. "We marked the start of the path to the root cellar by chiseling an *X* into a boulder. Then we moved it, so it would line up with the left corner of the house as we faced it from the trees."

After taking several more steps through the accumulation of fallen leaves, he stopped and studied the house. "We'll start here. If we find that boulder, then we should be able to locate the cellar entrance." He motioned for her to follow as he turned and walked into the thicket.

Bethany trailed behind him, swatting at low branches and underbrush while trying to keep up as he tramped deeper into the woods. Soon she heard rushing water and figured the stream must be close by. He walked several more feet, then stopped and pointed to a large rock with a crudely engraved "X" on its surface.

"Now we turn right."

He followed a narrow, overgrown path. When they had walked about ten feet, Bethany noticed a short stone wall covered with vegetation and spent foliage. Nick reached it first and pushed away the vines and brush to expose an aged wooden door almost flush with the ground.

"This is it." He eyed her expectantly. "Shall we go down?"

Bethany stared at the cellar entrance, trying to harness the courage to go forward. Although it was nothing more than an empty storage room, she was reluctant to venture down into the dark, musty, underground space. Old basements had never appealed to her, and this one was the epitome of unpleasant.

"Can you give me a minute?" she asked,

maintaining her distance from the entrance.

"Are you worried about encountering a ghost?"

"Of course not. I don't believe in ghosts. But…maybe it wouldn't hurt to check for other things. Rodents could be lurking down there. Or bugs."

"True. It might be a lair for giant spiders."

She looked up at Nick and frowned. "Okay. Now you're making fun of me."

"I'm sorry." He stepped closer and put his hand on her shoulder. "The old root cellar really isn't as creepy as it sounds."

"I know I'm being jumpy. It's just that I haven't been sleeping very well. I must be sensitive to the inn's quirks, like settling floorboards, rattling plumbing, and drafty windows. It's those things that are fueling my dreams about Samuel, not his ghost or spirit or any other paranormal entity."

"I get it." Nick slipped the backpack off his shoulders. "It's hard to admit that ghosts and spirits could exist. It sounds like something a crackpot would say. But…" He stopped, as if considering how to continue. "I've heard a lot of stories about paranormal experiences, especially those involving places like Horatio House, that made a believer out of me."

He sat on the stone wall, appearing to be in no hurry to open the door, and looked up at her.

"When we were kids, Zach and I were determined to either prove or discredit the haunted house rumors. Before the family renovated it, we regularly snuck inside Horatio House and poked around, hunting for ghosts."

"And I bet you didn't see anything strange." She sat down next to him.

"Well, we never saw a ghost. But something else

happened that convinced us the stories were true."

"Okay…" She eyed him. "I have to hear this."

"The summer I was twelve, Zach and I spent the night in Horatio House. We camped out on the floor with our sleeping bags and lanterns in the room where you're staying now. Neither of us could sleep, so we just lay there, nervous and scared. At one point, we heard tiny animals, like rats or mice, running across the floor."

"See, rodents *are* a thing."

He grinned. "Okay, you got me there. I'll admit that both of us zipped up our sleeping bags as far as we could without suffocating, even though it was a warm night."

She snickered at the thought of young, scared Nick completely encased in his sleeping bag.

"Eventually, I had to undo my sleeping bag and get some air. I don't know what time it was—neither of us had a watch—but I'm guessing it was an hour or two past midnight." He paused. "That's when it happened."

"When *what* happened?"

"We heard footsteps. Not the skittering of mice, but slow, heavy thumps. Like someone in work boots plodding along the wooden floor. They were faint at first, coming down the hallway, but grew louder and louder until we felt the vibration of the boards underneath us. That's when we knew something was outside the bedroom doorway. I was frantically zipping up my sleeping bag when the footsteps entered the room. The air suddenly got cold. Wintry cold. I could feel it through the sleeping bag. The presence in the room frightened me. But that wasn't the worst."

He stopped and absently swiped at a stray leaf resting on his thigh.

"Don't quit now." She poked him with her elbow.

"Tell me the rest."

"The footsteps grew louder, then stopped near my head. And that's when we heard the low-pitched moan echo throughout the room. It was like the cry of a large wounded animal groaning in agony, but different. Otherworldly. And so intense it bounced around the inside of my chest. My heart was pounding so hard I thought it would burst."

"Did you see who was walking?"

"No." Nick stared at a point beyond her, as if replaying the scene in his head. "I peeked through an opening in my sleeping bag but didn't see legs or feet. Zach didn't either. The thing was invisible. We lay there motionless for what seemed like forever while this spirit, or whatever it was, paced the room. Neither one of us dared to move. Finally, the moaning stopped, and it left. We both heard the footsteps move farther and farther away until they were gone. Even then, we didn't dare get out of our sleeping bags until it was light outside."

She shivered at Nick's description of the sound. He was describing what she heard in her dream: the thumping of Samuel's work boots on the polished wood floor in her bedroom and his eerie, unearthly moan.

"Maybe you dreamed it. You didn't realize you'd fallen asleep. Since your senses were on high alert, your mind invented the entire experience."

He held her gaze. "Not every paranormal encounter is a dream. And honestly, I doubt your encounters with Samuel are just dreams. I'm sure they're real interactions with a spirit…a ghost. I wish you were more open to accepting that."

"And I wish you would acknowledge that our brains conjure these encounters." She pressed her lips into a tight line to avoid saying something she'd regret. Why was he so hell-bent on turning her into a believer? She didn't want to argue with him, but his words irritated her.

Nick's expression softened. "I know our beliefs are worlds apart when it comes to the paranormal. But can we agree to disagree?" He pushed at the wayward lock of brown hair on his forehead, then rested his hand on hers. "I don't want a difference of opinion to come between us."

Her skin tingled and her heart pounded from his touch. Immediately, she regretted her sharp tone. Although his ghost talk was irksome, she enjoyed his company and didn't want to jeopardize their friendship. Or destroy the possibility of taking it to the next level, a thought that kept popping into her head despite an all-out effort to curb any romantic hankering for him.

Owen had never affected her like this. He was practical, the type of man who'd mapped out his life— including their relationship and probably his affair, too—into five-year increments. She'd strode into that romance with a clear head and steady pulse because she'd believed sharing a life with Owen was the sensible, safe thing to do. And it had blown up in her face.

Falling for Nick wasn't sensible or safe. He was handsome and irresistible, but exasperating and opinionated. He'd broken her heart before and could do it again. But there was also a chance that he wouldn't.

"Me, either," she mumbled. "Friends wouldn't let that happen."

Before she could react, Nick wrapped his arm around her shoulders and drew her against him. "I agree. Friends wouldn't do that. And we're friends, right?"

"Yep, we are. Just friends."

"But I wouldn't mind if…" He paused, pulling her closer as he took a deep breath. "If we explored being more than friends."

Her thoughts whirled as she instinctively leaned against him, her resolution to stay strong wavering. She wouldn't mind being more than friends either. Actually, she'd like it a lot. Before considering being "more than friends" though, she needed to find out why he had ghosted her. And she needed to tell him about Owen. He should know about her broken engagement.

But his hug felt amazing. And soon the desire to nestle in closer—capture the warmth of his chest; breathe in his warm, salty scent; touch his cheek; taste his lips; be here with him in this embrace all day—replaced all her rational thoughts. But none of that could happen. She wasn't ready to be more than friends. Not yet. There were things she needed to know. Things he needed to know. Maybe now was the right time to ask. And tell.

Reluctantly, she leaned away and searched his face. His eyes radiated tenderness, and the courage she'd mustered to launch a serious conversation faded away as she resisted the urge to drift back into his arms.

"You are very good at distracting me, Nick Dorsey," she said, forcing a playful grin while extricating herself from his hold. "However, if I remember correctly, we're on a mission and I have a point to prove." She stood and motioned to the wooden door beside them. "Are you ready to find nothing in the root cellar?"

Nick reached down, grabbed his backpack, and grasped the rusty ring fastened to the front of the door. The hinges groaned as he pulled on it, and then the door flung open to reveal a gaping black hole and deteriorating stone stairs that disappeared into an abyss.

He turned back to her, his face unreadable.

"Ready," he replied.

****

Bethany peered into the opaque void. "It's so dark."

"Good thing I brought some light." Nick pulled out two large camping flashlights from his backpack, switched them on, and handed one to Bethany. "Be careful. The stones in the steps may be loose."

With a deep breath, Bethany followed Nick. As soon as her foot touched the second step, a surge of frigid air swept past her. She shivered and exhaled. A cloud of fog hovered near her nose and cheeks as she slowly advanced down the narrow stairway.

Ahead of her, Nick's tall form dominated the room as he directed his flashlight around the space. The bright beam illuminated the rough stone walls and low, arched ceiling, as well as rotting wooden shelves supported by cinder blocks. In the shadows, the space felt massive, although it was about the size of a small bedroom.

Nick swung his flashlight toward Bethany and set it down in the dirt, his body fading into the dimness as his beam lit the area between their feet. "The air smells stale," he said, coughing. "I doubt anyone's been down here since I was a kid."

The earthy scent, a mixture of decaying leaves and wet dog fur, didn't bother Bethany. But the damp cold permeated her skin and settled into her bones. She expected they would leave the root cellar in a few minutes and she'd warm up in the sunlight. Instead, Nick dropped his backpack and pulled something out. She focused her light on the dirt floor and saw he'd brought a garden trowel, hand rake, and two pairs of gloves.

"What's all that for?" Bethany blurted out,

astonished. "Surely you're not planning to dig up the root cellar."

Nick looked up. His face, illuminated by her flashlight, registered surprise. "How else will we find Samuel?"

"We won't. Because his body isn't here. He fell overboard and his remains are at the bottom of the bay, somewhere between Matapeake Beach and the Annapolis Harbor dock."

He shrugged. "Maybe he's here. Or maybe not. We won't know for sure unless we look."

Bethany's stomach clenched at the thought of combing through the dirt for Samuel's bones. She aimed her flashlight at the floor again, imagining Samuel's skull with empty eye sockets, lifeless and unseeing, staring up at her, and was hit with a wave of revulsion.

"I'd rather not. It sounds like a lot of work just to prove I'm right."

"Then how about a compromise? We do the search. And if our efforts are unsuccessful, I'll concede that Samuel's spirit doesn't roam Horatio House. That ghosts aren't real. And your imagination is fueling your dreams."

"Uh, I don't think so."

Suddenly, the temperature dropped, as though someone opened a freezer door, and frigid, lavender-scented air swirled across her face and arms.

"I'm here. Find me. I beg you."

The words, barely audible, floated past her and disappeared as though never spoken. Shuddering, Bethany jerked her light up and looked at Nick.

"Did you say something?"

He studied her. "No."

She sighed. Now she was hearing voices down here, too.

"However…" Nick's lips curved into his boyish grin, but the shadows obscured his features so that he appeared more spectral than human. "I was about to plead with you to help me look for Samuel's remains."

Did she want to dig around down here? Not at all. This place was way too creepy. And cold. However, spending more time with him *would* give her a chance to find out what happened at the end of that summer and bring up her broken engagement with Owen. Maybe even explore the idea of being more than friends with Nick. And squashing his ghost theory was a plus.

"Well, I might be persuaded if we make the stakes more interesting. You know, sweeten the spoils."

His smile widened, and his teeth gleamed white against the shadows that darkened his face. "What'd you have in mind?"

"When we *don't* find anything, you can never mention ghosts or spirits to me again. Ever. *And* you're on the hook for a four-course dinner at the restaurant of my choice. With no restrictions."

"And what do I get when we *do* find something?" he asked with a smirk.

"You can talk about ghosts all you want and I'll buy you a four-course dinner at the restaurant of your choice. No restrictions."

"Deal."

He thrust his hand toward her, and she grasped his palm. His warm touch sent a spark that fired up every nerve ending in her body. She quickly released it.

"We should start with a plan," she said. "Unless you want to scratch around willy-nilly."

He scanned the root cellar with his flashlight, then walked to the far wall and back.

"We need to be careful, so we don't damage Samuel's remains. How about one of us loosens the dirt with the hand rake while the other turns it over with the trowel?" He pushed the small rake toward her with his foot and tossed her a pair of gardening gloves. "If you'll start raking, I'll dig. We can switch off later."

"Sure," she answered, working to keep her voice steady. Clearly there was no chance of finding Samuel's remains. His murder was a fabrication, something she'd dreamed up, right? With a shiver, she wriggled her fingers into the gloves. They warmed her hands but did little to ease the apprehension that gripped her chest as she picked up the rake.

"You're cold. Here, wear this." Nick removed his coat and pulled off his red Maryland hoodie, revealing a thick crew-neck sweater underneath.

The sweatshirt was large enough to cover her jacket. She slipped it over her head and inhaled the salty scent. It smelled like the sea. Like Nick. She crossed her arms, wrapping herself in his essence, and hoped the shadows would hide the flush that flooded her cheeks. Digging down here with Nick, as friends, wouldn't be easy. To stay in control of her wits, she needed to maintain a clear head and concentrate on the task at hand.

"We should identify a starting point," she said, walking to the center of the root cellar. "If Frederick *had* dragged Samuel down the steps, which he didn't, he probably would have pulled him a foot or so into the room before dropping him." She pointed to a spot in the middle of the floor.

"Okay. Good point."

She eyed the space. "And then Frederick would have dug a burial pit next to the body and rolled it into the hole. So we should map out two plots. One left and one right of the spot where Frederick likely dropped him." Bethany lifted a brow as she motioned to the floor. "We can use your body as a guide."

"Fantastic," Nick muttered as he lay on his back about a foot from the stairwell and midway between the two side walls. Bethany kneeled on his right and, starting at his feet, used the hand rake to mark the perimeter of a two-foot-wide plot. As she moved along his torso, she heard his breathing and sensed the warmth radiating from his skin. She scanned his body as she worked, extremely aware of the way it had filled out over the years, with a sturdier build replacing his teenage lankiness. When she reached his shoulders, he glanced at her. Although the shadows masked his expression, she could make out the shape of his face with its defined jawline and cheek bones. It, too, had also matured.

Aside from the physical changes, this older version of Nick wasn't much different from the Nick she'd known ten years ago. Her gaze lingered on his body as she moved to the other side of his head to etch out a plot on his left, and a touch of sadness squeezed her chest. She'd missed this. Hanging out with him, embracing new projects, and experiencing life. They'd been so close. Was it even possible to recapture what they had?

She finished marking the dirt floor and lightly poked his foot. "I'm done. You can get up now."

Nick scrambled to his feet. "So, we're doing this?"

She studied the two rectangles outlined in the dirt, and her thoughts turned to Samuel. The idea that Frederick Howard buried him alive weighed on her heart. It would have been a brutal way for him to die, especially when carried out by a man who'd coveted his wife and claimed to be the father of his son. She couldn't imagine the pain and agony it would have caused. Enough to keep Samuel's spirit trapped in Horatio House?

No. It was absurd to believe his remains were down here. Ghosts didn't exist. Her overactive imagination had created this scenario. Samuel fell overboard traveling to Annapolis, and the only thing beneath the cellar's dirt floor was more dirt.

"Bethany?" Nick's voice broke into her thoughts.

"Yes. We're absolutely doing this. And I'm looking forward to the dinner *you'll* be buying."

Chapter 10: Foul Play in the Root Cellar, Part 2

They started digging in the plot on the left. Bethany hacked at the compacted soil and Nick scooped and turned the loosened dirt with the hand trowel. The earth was a mix of sand, bits of clay, and sediment, making it an easy task to break up the surface into mounds of pea-size clumps with the hand rake's short, stubby tines.

"How deep do you think we'll need to dig?" she asked.

"I'd say twelve inches. Six at the very least."

"It'll take hours to sift through all this dirt."

He chuckled. "Probably."

They fell into an easy silence. As she raked, Bethany glanced sideways at Nick. Would she be able to ask him why he disappeared after that last summer? Or tell him about Owen? Her stomach tightened as she thought about what to say. *I never heard from you and it broke my heart. Eventually, I got engaged but discovered my fiancé cheated on me, so I canceled the wedding, then came here to nurse my wounds. And now, I'm starting to fall for you again, and it frightens me because I can't survive another round of emotional pain if you ghost me like you did before.*

"Nick," she said, breaking the stillness. "What happened…" Her throat constricted and she stopped, unable to get her words out. Why couldn't she just ask him? What did she have to lose?

He stopped sifting and looked over at her. Although the shadows obscured his face, she could make out the question in his eyes. She inhaled and tried again.

"After you graduated from high school?" She lost her nerve and silently cursed her lack of courage. "You mentioned you were a marine scientist. How did you get into that?"

"Oh." He turned back to the floor and continued working. "I didn't know what to study in college, so I picked something that sounded fun, as well as useful. Which led me to classes on environmental science. I ended up studying the Chesapeake Bay."

"You always loved the water. I remember you'd spend every minute on the beach or the bay if you could."

"Still do," he said, grinning.

"I believe it." She snickered as she scraped the dirt.

"And what about you? How did you end up being a fancy corporate fundraiser?"

"I loved language arts. Reading. Writing. Research. For me, composing papers is like putting together a jigsaw puzzle. Once I collect all the information, it's just a matter of fitting it into the right spot."

"I didn't know you liked to write."

"I do. It led me to a communications degree. And I discovered I was good at nonfiction."

"Like newspaper articles?"

"More like researching and writing things such as grant proposals, fundraising campaigns, and donor programs."

He paused to study her. "That makes sense."

They shared work stories while maneuvering around each other in the tiny plot. She described galas she'd planned for the Institute, and he listed various fish species found in the Chesapeake Bay. The conversation boosted Bethany's mood, leaving her confident they could work side by side without distraction.

And then his arm brushed against her shoulder.

Despite the sweatshirt, jacket, and sweater covering her skin, Bethany's heart thumped wildly at his touch. She flinched, rattled by her reaction, and checked her watch. Only an hour and a half had passed since they started scratching at the dirt, and she was already swooning over the slightest contact with him. Worse, they weren't even close to finishing. The undisturbed portion of the plot she'd drawn loomed in front of her, a guarantee that several more hours of raking and sifting lay ahead.

To clear her thoughts, she stood to stretch out the aches in her shoulders, back, and knees. Nick stopped sifting and looked up at her.

"You okay?" he asked.

"Just a little stiff."

"Me, too." He rose and surveyed their progress. "Digging on my hands and knees isn't as easy as I thought it'd be."

She groaned. "And slower."

"Is it too much for you?"

"I can keep going." Bethany shot Nick a challenging look. "How about you? Or have you concluded we're chasing after an illusion and are ready to call it quits?"

He lifted a brow and shook his head. "No way. I'm planning on having a fancy dinner, compliments of *you*."

"All right, then. Let's get back to finding nothing."

They resumed raking and sifting until Nick broke the stillness.

"It's odd that Samuel and Frederick ended up in a

knife fight. He told you they were going to attend the meeting about the merchant smuggling British tea. Would they fight about that? I'd think they'd be politically aligned."

"I'm afraid my political knowledge of the era is horribly lacking," she replied. "But my gut…supported by the dreams fabricated by my subconscious mind and not a spirit haunting me…tells me they fought over Ariella."

"Ah. Because Samuel thought they were having an affair?"

She shrugged and kept raking. "Isn't love the reason why men usually fight over women in the first place? *If* Samuel and Frederick actually had a fight, that is."

"Yep. Because of jealousy and rage. Samuel must have heard or seen something that fired up his temper."

"Like Frederick trying to woo Ariella."

He stopped sifting and snorted. "Did you just say *woo*?"

She scowled. "What's wrong with that?"

He snickered. "It sounds like something you'd read in one of those steamy historical romance novels. Natalie Rose used to read those and, believe it or not, she talked me into reading one. Once." He laughed again. "I never pictured you as a hopeless romantic. More like the love 'em and leave 'em type."

Did he really just say that?

Bethany stopped, wounded by his comment. "What's that supposed to mean?"

Okay, she'd sidestepped his earlier declaration of wanting to be more than friends. But she'd insisted from the start they were friends only, so he should understand why she'd shut down the moments between them that could have led to more. Besides, if anyone should be accused of loving and leaving, it was him. After all, he was the one who'd left *her* hanging, all those years ago.

Nick looked away as she peered at him through the dimness. She waited for him to reply, impatient to hear his answer. But the stillness stretched into an awkward silence. Wasn't he going to explain? Or… Wait. Did he think she was a tease?

Suddenly tired, Bethany laid the rake in the dirt and stood. "Maybe coming down here was a bad idea. I'm going back to the inn."

As she walked toward the cellar steps, a gust of cold air rushed through the underground chamber. It penetrated her shoulders and, as if possessing her, slithered down her spine to her hips and legs. Shivering, Bethany folded her arms across her chest.

"You can't leave. I need your help."

The voice was clearer this time. Like someone was down here with them. Stunned, Bethany turned to Nick. "Did you hear that?"

Nick looked up at her, his face stony. "That you're going back to the inn? Yes, I heard you loud and clear."

"That's not—"

"You have the power to reveal my fate. I'm certain of it."

The voice—louder, urgent, and pleading—filled her skull. A flash of intense heat replaced the chill that overtook her earlier, and tiny specks of bright light clouded her vision. Her head throbbed.

"Find my signet ring. It'll lead you to me. You must continue searching. Pleeeease…"

The last word mutated into a wail. The ache in her temples intensified until it was a sharp, stabbing pain.

She clutched her head and dropped to her knees, certain she would topple otherwise.

"Bethany?" Nick scrambled to her side, his eyes filled with concern. "What's happening?"

"That sound. Don't you hear it?" She clamped her palms over her ears, trying to ease the agony caused by the continuous bass note permeating her brain. Cramps squeezed her gut, and she doubled over, resting her head on her forearms while gasping for breath.

Nick moved next to her and gently laid his palm against her forehead. "We need to get you back to Horatio House. Can you stand?" Without waiting for a response, he lodged his shoulder under her arm and pulled her to her feet. Then he placed his arm around her waist for support and helped her up the stone stairs.

Bethany sagged against Nick when they stepped out into the thicket, breathing deeply to replace the cellar's dankness with fresh, fall-scented air. The howling in her head quieted, and the sharp pain subsided into a dull, throbbing ache.

"Are you okay?" He looked down at her with a mix of alarm and worry, then tightened his supporting grip. "You said you heard something."

"You didn't hear it?"

"No. What did it sound like?"

She rubbed her temple and straightened. "I don't know. A low-pitched moan, maybe. But intense. I thought my head was going to explode."

It made no sense. The sound had reverberated through her head, growing stronger and stronger until she left the root cellar. But Nick was completely unaffected. He hadn't heard it at all, which baffled her even more.

"Did you hear anything else?"

She shook her head, deciding not to mention the voice that accompanied the moan. "It was probably a draft whistling through the door. That's all. And for some reason, it gave me a headache, but I'm better now."

"Are you good to walk back to the inn?"

She nodded and leaned on Nick as he led her out of the woods toward Horatio House with his arm wrapped firmly around her waist the entire way.

*****

Mrs. Snowden eyed Bethany with concern as she set a cup of hot tea in front of her. "You really should go upstairs and lie down, dear. You're still as white as a sheet."

Bethany swallowed the brew, grateful for its soothing warmth. She'd downed two ibuprofen tablets, and the headache had softened to a slight pulse behind her eyes. Feeling more like herself, she mulled over Nick's love 'em and leave 'em comment. Now that he'd made his impression of her perfectly clear, she could move forward knowing she'd never be more than his friend.

Mrs. Snowden scrutinized her a minute longer before turning to Nick. "I hope you two aren't planning to go back there."

"We're not." His reply was immediate.

We're not? Bethany stood and stared at Nick with surprise. He'd started this ghost hunt, and now she was determined to see it through and prove, with or without him, that she wasn't being haunted by Samuel's spirit.

"Well, I'd like to go back. I'm fine now."

Mrs. Snowden shook her head. "I don't think you should venture down there again."

"Aunt Margaret has a point." Nick's brown eyes flashed as he scowled at Bethany. "If I take you and something happens, I'll have to deal with her wrath for the rest of my life. That's just too high a price to pay."

"I appreciate your concern, but this is something I want to do, and I'm sure I can find the root cellar again on my own." Bethany walked toward the back door. "I have a bet to win."

Nick grasped Bethany's arm. "Then wait until tomorrow and get some rest now, okay?" His scowl softened, replaced by another expression Bethany tried to identify. Apprehension? "I'd never forgive myself if something happened to you."

"Okay. Tomorrow then."

She sighed. He was being overprotective, but it wasn't worth an argument. Since the root cellar was on the inn's property, she understood why Mrs. Snowden would object to her going back. But Nick? He'd suggested they dig there in the first place.

"Nick, you'll go with her, right?" Mrs. Snowden asked.

He lifted his brows and directed his gaze at Bethany. "I will if Bethany wants me to tag along. It's her decision."

Bethany shrugged, not wanting Mrs. Snowden to worry. "That's fine with me."

"Then how about we start early," he replied. "Around nine?"

Bethany nodded. "Sure."

"And Bethany," Mrs. Snowden added, "if you feel a headache coming, you'll leave immediately, right?"

"Absolutely." She turned to Nick. "I'll see you tomorrow morning."

Before he could reply, Bethany left the kitchen and hurried upstairs. Once inside her room, she plopped into the chair by the fireplace and stared at the cold embers in the hearth while sorting out the events in the root cellar.

She must have had some sort of weird waking dream. The man's voice sounded like Samuel's, and the words sounded clearer each time he spoke. But none of it was real. Her mind had fabricated everything—the dreams, his voice in the root cellar—and the effort had cost her. She'd never experienced such an intense headache before. The pain today had been excruciating, something she never wanted to endure again. Ever.

So why was she so intent on returning to the root cellar tomorrow? Nick was reluctant to go back there, and digging for Samuel's remains was futile. Was it worth dragging Nick back just to prove a point?

No.

She'd let him know tomorrow morning that their bet was off and there was no reason to continue the search.

A glance at the clock showed it was still early afternoon. Plenty of time to grab a nap before dinner with Aunt Ginny. Bethany set her phone timer for two hours and crawled into the bed.

Chapter 11: Maybe Ghosts *Are* Real

"I fried up some chicken and made an apple pie to celebrate the occasion," Aunt Ginny said, pulling Bethany into a hug before ushering her into the tiny living room. The Queen Street bungalow had barely changed since Bethany's last visit. A creamy white leather sofa, accented with soft pink pillows, stood between the room's tall, narrow windows. The fireplace blazed with yellow flames, and the aroma of cinnamon and nutmeg wafted through the room.

After a studied glance, Aunt Ginny hooked her arm around Bethany's and led her to the dining room table. "You look tired, hon. Sit here so we can talk while I finish mashing the potatoes."

Bethany took a seat and scanned the room as Aunt Ginny retreated into the kitchen. Ten years had passed since Bethany last ate dinner here. But it seemed like only days since she'd sat on this high-back dining chair, drinking iced tea, eating apple pie, and discussing school and boys with Aunt Ginny and Sarah.

"I looked at the history festival packet and made some comments," Bethany said. She fished a folder out of her bag, along with the borrowed library book, and laid them on the table. "I brought it with me."

Aunt Ginny set a plateful of food in front of Bethany. "You're an angel. Do you mind if I look at your notes later?"

"Sounds good to me." Bethany grinned. "Your fried chicken deserves our full attention. It's always been my favorite. And you timed the dinner invitation perfectly. My day was a bit on the stressful side."

"Poor dear. I have just the thing. Grandma Day's favorite remedy for someone who's feeling outta sorts."

Aunt Ginny retrieved a bottle of whiskey and sweet vermouth from a cabinet in the kitchen and mixed a Manhattan for each of them. "So what made your day so rough? Did Nick Dorsey have something to do with it?"

A sigh escaped Bethany's lips. "We butted heads over something. And we were working on agreeing to disagree. But then everything fell apart."

With a sympathetic cluck, Aunt Ginny set a cocktail in front of Bethany. "Why don't you start at the beginning?"

Bethany reached for the drink and gulped down a mouthful, nervous about sharing everything that had happened. Would Aunt Ginny, like Nick, push the notion that Samuel was haunting her?

"Nick takes the inn's reputation as a haunted house very seriously, and he's convinced I'm being haunted by Samuel Watts."

Aunt Ginny frowned. "That's quite an assumption. Why does he think that?"

Before she lost her nerve, Bethany described everything since her first dream about Samuel, except where she and Nick took Samuel's claim to the next level and, against her better judgment, started digging around in the root cellar to find him. She'd save that confession for later.

"I just don't believe I'm being haunted, Aunt Ginny. For me, accepting ghosts are real is like declaring fairies, dragons, and unicorns exist. But Nick keeps bringing it up, which is extremely annoying."

Aunt Ginny leaned in, her eyes thoughtful. "I appreciate how you feel, but I think you should give Nick some leeway. His family owns Horatio House. It has a reputation for being haunted, and he's been hearing the ghost stories since he was a kid. I bet he's encountered things you and I can't even imagine."

"Still, there are other, more reasonable explanations for strange dreams."

"Not always. Some things just defy logic."

Bethany frowned. *Not you, too, Aunt Ginny.* "Please don't tell me you believe in ghosts."

"Oh, sweetie, of course I do." Aunt Ginny swirled the ice in her drink. "I've experienced odd, unexplainable occurrences here all my life. It doesn't matter what anyone says or believes. I know ghosts exist. Not just here in town, but all over the Eastern Shore. There's no denying it."

Aunt Ginny walked over to the buffet and retrieved a slim book from the display shelf and handed it to Bethany. "This has information on the Eastern Shore's hauntings, which you might find interesting. It includes a write-up on the Horatio House ghost."

Bethany eyed the cover. "Ghostly Sightings in Queen Anne's County" was stamped in gold leaf on the faded burgundy leather. Great. Now Aunt Ginny was pushing the ghost thing on her. She held in a sigh.

"People have reported ghostly incidents on the Eastern Shore for centuries," Aunt Ginny continued. "The people who lived here before us faced many hardships that often led to heartache and despair. I think most of them, when the time came, welcomed their journey to wherever the afterlife takes us. But some souls weren't able to move forward. They lingered here, trapped by their emotional state, and sought solace among the living."

Bethany bit her lip to hide a smirk. "Aunt Ginny, are you telling me you've seen ghosts?"

Her aunt shook her head. "No, but I've sensed them. Felt the prickle of cold air on the back of my neck, and the phantom touch on my shoulder. I've smelled traces of lavender, and pipe tobacco. Heard the whispers of children laughing and echoes of women crying." She paused and pursed her lips. "And I've seen firsthand what happens when people are being haunted."

Silence hung over the table as Bethany studied her aunt. "I'm sorry, Aunt Ginny, but I have to believe there's always a credible reason for even the strangest occurrence. And being haunted isn't one of them."

"Hold on." Suspicion washed over Aunt Ginny's features as she eyed Bethany. "You experienced something at Horatio House besides those dreams, didn't you?"

"Well, it wasn't a ghostly encounter." Keeping secrets from Aunt Ginny wasn't her strong suit, so Bethany told her about digging in the root cellar that morning, the low-pitched wailing sound, and her subsequent headache.

Aunt Ginny scowled. "I'm not thrilled that you're poking around in that old cellar. Or staying at Horatio House, for that matter. I'd rather you were here."

"Please don't worry. I'm not planning to go back to the root cellar. And if I get spooked at the inn, which is unlikely, I'll come right over. I promise."

"I'm holding you to that." Aunt Ginny stood and

gathered their empty plates. "Did you know a spirit haunted your mom?"

What? That couldn't be true. It was unthinkable. Her mother was one of the most practical, level-headed people she knew.

"No way, Aunt Ginny. You're messing with me."

"It happened while we were growing up."

Bethany stared at her aunt. "Mom never said anything."

"I'm not surprised. The whole thing rattled her. It was the reason she left Worthington Cove. And your dad went with her."

They left because Mom thought she encountered a spirit? Nope. Absolutely not. Her parents moved away because they were tired of living in a small town. They wanted more opportunities. A better life.

"That's just hard to believe. They wouldn't move away because of what…strange sounds? Cold air?"

"Oh, much more than that." Aunt Ginny motioned toward Bethany's empty tumbler. "Want another Manhattan?"

"Will I need one?"

Aunt Ginny's expression lightened, and she chuckled. "Probably."

Bethany followed her aunt into the kitchen with the empty cocktail glasses. "If you'll make the drinks, I'll do the dishes."

"You've got a deal." Aunt Ginny pulled two fresh glasses out of the cabinet and started pouring the whiskey. "The house where your mom, Jacob, and I grew up was called Cornelius Day House."

Bethany wiped off the plates and stowed them in the dishwasher. "That's Grandma and Grandpa Day's house.

Where Uncle Jacob lives now."

"I always thought it was pretentious that our house had a name, but it's part of the town's history. Your great-great-grandfather, Cornelius Day, built it in the eighteen sixties. Grandpa Day and his older sister, Edwina, grew up there, too." Aunt Ginny cut two slices of apple pie, then tipped her head toward the living room. "Let's sit by the fire. Can you grab the drinks?"

Bethany followed and settled onto the sofa. "So tell me about my mom's experience."

"Aunt Edwina's ghost tormented her. For years."

Bethany almost gagged on a mouthful of pie. "Her ghost?"

"She'd show up while Cat was asleep."

"Like, in a dream?"

"I suppose. Cat said the encounters were realistic, as though Edwina was right there in the room with her. Like your dreams with Samuel Watts, I imagine. The visits were infrequent at first—they started when she was in elementary school—but recurred more often as she got older. When Cat was in high school, Edwina dropped in almost every night."

"Did Mom ever describe her dreams?"

"She said Edwina was a talker, and would drone on and on about people she knew and places she'd been. And she also talked about the war. Cat was like a walking time capsule from the nineteen forties, spouting information about the current events back then, as well as cars, clothes, singers, and movie stars that were popular at the time. More than once, Cat stunned Grandpa Day with details from the past that Edwina had told her. Things she wouldn't know otherwise."

A shudder passed through Bethany's shoulders. If

her mom's dreams with Edwina were anything like her dreams with Samuel, they probably left her worn-out. But that didn't mean she was haunted.

"Mom probably heard people talking. That's how she knew things. Kids hear a lot more than adults realize. They're experts at eavesdropping."

"That may be true. But not in your mom's case. Edwina hounded that poor girl. Apparently, she was lonely. When she discovered your mom was someone she could interact with, she seized the opportunity to tell her everything. The rest of us—me, Jacob, Grandma, and Grandpa—never experienced a visit. I don't think we're wired to detect paranormal activity. But apparently Cat is. And Edwina latched onto her and held on tight."

Aunt Ginny paused and took a breath. "Eventually, Edwina's incessant chatter wore your mom down. At one point, just before her high school graduation, Cat had become so gaunt and haggard that Grandma and I worried she'd fall over from exhaustion. Grandma took her to the doctor, but he couldn't find anything wrong. That's when we knew her health issues stemmed from Edwina's spirit disrupting her sleep. There was no other explanation."

"So Mom left because of Edwina?"

"Cat only found peace when she was away from Day House. She'd spend the night with friends as often as she could, but it wasn't enough to really help. So as soon as she finished high school, she married your dad and moved to Oklahoma."

Bethany inhaled as she processed the story. She couldn't imagine that version of her mother.

"Did Grandpa tell you how Edwina died?"

"He was around thirteen years old when Edwina

passed away. She was twenty. The Japanese had just bombed Pearl Harbor, which drew the United States into World War II. Her fiancé, Earl Hammond, enlisted in the Navy. A lot of our hometown boys did. Earl ended up stationed in Europe, and the stress from his deployment and waiting weeks for his letters or other news was too much for Edwina. To help her sleep, the doctor prescribed a barbiturate. One night, she took too much and died from an overdose."

"Oh, wow. That's so sad. But I'm not convinced Edwina haunted my mom. Something else caused those dreams. Maybe she was anxious. High school can be very stressful."

"Think what you will, but Cat knows she's sensitive to ghosts, spirits, or whatever you want to call them. It's not something she talks about, but she avoids situations where she might experience one. Whenever you all came back to Worthington Cove, she never went near Day House."

"Okay, she had trouble sleeping there. But—"

"To me, it's pretty clear you're sensitive to them, too." Concern clouded Aunt Ginny's eyes. "That's why I worry about you staying at Horatio House. And if Cat knew you were there, she'd be apprehensive, too."

"I'm not a ghost whisperer, Aunt Ginny, and Mom isn't either." She gulped the rest of her Manhattan. "My issue is a very active imagination, nothing more. I'll be fine, I swear."

Frowning, Aunt Ginny shook her head. "Like you were this morning?"

Bethany poked at her apple pie with the fork. "That was a fluke. Probably from the wind gusting through rotten sections of the cellar door. But I won't be down there again, so there's no need to worry."

Aunt Ginny drained her glass. "I wouldn't be so sure. That property has a ghost. He's attached himself to you, and he wants your help."

****

Back in her room at the inn, Bethany nestled underneath the thick quilts. All she'd wanted was to get over Owen and move forward. So how'd she end up involved in this ghost drama? She wasn't sensitive to spirits. It was impossible, because ghosts didn't exist. No matter what Nick and Aunt Ginny said.

Still, curiosity about the hauntings reported at Horatio House tugged at her brain. She retrieved Aunt Ginny's ghostly sightings book from the nightstand and flipped through the yellowed pages, stopping to read the text when she saw the entries for Worthington Cove. She read:

Most notable is the ghost who besieges Horatio House. Reportedly, the soul roaming the building haunts the occupants with heavy footsteps during the night; frigid drafts; slamming doors; the sense of being touched; lingering aromas of lavender, tobacco, and burning wood; and a voice that sobs and cries. Residents also report knives mysteriously disappear, only to reappear in plain view days later.

Unconvinced, Bethany closed the book and switched off the lamp. Although stories supporting the ghostly activity were abundant, they were still conjecture. Theories without proof. Unless there was solid evidence to back up the assertions, which was inconceivable, she'd remain an unbeliever. Satisfied with her resolution, she pulled the bedcovers close to her chin and fell asleep almost immediately.

"Why did you leave the cellar? I waited for you to come back. But you never returned."

The words, vibrating with accusation, seeped through the quilts and invaded Bethany's sleeping mind. She stirred, recognizing Samuel's voice as he asked another question.

"Is it your plan to make me suffer for all eternity?"

"Quit being so dramatic," she mumbled sleepily. "Besides, you're just a dream. And an annoying one at that. Go away and don't bother me anymore."

Tendrils of icy air brushed Bethany's cheek, chasing away the last traces of her drowsiness. She peeked from under the layers of covers and scowled. Samuel stood by her bed. His handsome face was pale, and the corners of his mouth turned downward as though weighted by centuries of suffering. His forlorn demeanor pricked her heart. Although he was an illusion, she empathized with the man who claimed he'd lost his life at the hands of his wife's first love.

"Don't admonish me, Miss Bethany," he murmured. "Since you're getting close to discovering my resting place, I'm compelled to ensure you continue your search."

"Samuel—"

"I'm wearing my ring. It will provide evidence that the body buried there is mine."

"Samuel, your body isn't down there. You were lost at sea and your remains are lying somewhere beneath the Chesapeake Bay. Now let me go back to sleep."

The mattress wobbled, and she peeked through half-opened lids to find him perched on the bed.

"You're mistaken. I *am* there. And you must uncover my remains, as I have no one else to bring my murder to light."

"I left the root cellar yesterday because something gave me a terrible headache. And I'm not going back." Her tone was dismissive as she shut her eyes. "Besides, there's nothing to find since you aren't buried there."

"Don't say that. You must believe me. Miss Bethany, I beg of you. Pleeeease…"

The word distorted into a moan, and a wave of pain crashed into Bethany's head. Trembling, she sat up and inched away from him.

"That sound!" She groaned, covering her ears. "It's hurting me. You have to stop!"

Abruptly, he closed his mouth. When he spoke again, his voice was subdued and filled with concern. "The pain you felt in the cellar. Could I have caused it?"

She rubbed her temples. "I'm sure it was a strong draft blowing through the root cellar that made something vibrate. That's the only explanation."

"No," he murmured, his voice tinged with sadness. "I'm certain the sound you heard came from me." He reached over and laid his hand on her forearm. When she stiffened at his touch, he withdrew his hand.

"You were giving up on the search," he continued, "and I couldn't bear the thought of you leaving me down there. So I started howling like a damned lout, and you suffered because of it. Harming you is inexcusable."

Frowning, he reached behind his head and untied the ribbon holding his hair. Then he leaned over and knotted the slender slip of black fabric around her wrist to form a bracelet. She was staring at her arm, startled by his gentleness, when he brushed the top of her hand with a soft, wintry kiss.

"What are you doing?"

"This is a token of my intention. I'm giving you my word that I'll manage my grief during our interactions and refrain from tormenting you with my sobs or sighs."

She pulled her hand away and drew the quilt to her chin. "I'd rather you stay out of my head altogether."

"Ah, but I can't, Miss Bethany. Don't you see that fate has brought us together? It's your destiny to find me, and my destiny to be found by you. It's why we have this connection."

He studied her, his gaze determined. "Therefore, I cannot abandon my affiliation with you until we've achieved the purpose of our union, which is to uncover my remains in the root cellar and bring my murder to light. But you can rest assured I will remain stoic and suppress my outbursts accordingly. This is my pledge to you."

Oh, great. An ongoing connection with you. Just what I need.

Sighing, she burrowed deeper beneath the quilts, turning away from the man who wouldn't leave her alone, and resigned herself to resuming the search in the root cellar.

****

Bethany grudgingly grasped the corners of the quilts and slowly cast them aside, willing herself to rise and acknowledge the morning. Instead of getting up, though, she lay on the bed and stared up at the ceiling, leaving her exhausted, pajama-clad body exposed to the morning chill in the room. The thought of returning to the root cellar and scratching around in the dirt only exacerbated her weariness. If her mother's dreams about Edwina had left her this tired, she understood why Aunt Ginny thought Cat was haunted.

When the aroma of fresh-brewed coffee wafted into her room, she sat up with a groan and ran a hand through her hair. As she lowered her arm, she spotted something on her wrist from the corner of her eye.

Tied there, like a bracelet, was a shabby, faded black ribbon.

Holy shit.

Her heart pounded furiously. It couldn't be.

She must still be asleep, and this had to be a dream. Why else was that ribbon—Samuel's hair tie—wrapped around her wrist? She squeezed her eyes shut. Surely, when she opened them, she'd be awake and the ribbon would be gone.

Slowly, she raised an eyelid, scanned her wrist, and saw it. *I'm still dreaming.*

Bethany quickly unfastened the knot, flicked the piece of fabric away from her skin, and climbed out of bed. She washed her face, brushed her teeth, and combed the snarls out of her hair. Now confident she was awake, Bethany stepped into the bedroom and glanced at the bed.

The ribbon was there, lying where it had landed on top of the quilt. She turned her back to the bed, got dressed, then glanced in the mirror at the quilt. The tie was still there.

This couldn't be happening.

She focused on breathing as she racked her brain for an explanation. Maybe it belonged to the previous guest, and she'd somehow dislodged it from the headboard. Or the housekeeper left it while cleaning the room. Both were plausible causes for its presence.

Except neither explained how it came to be tied around her wrist.

Frowning, she reached over and smoothed out the inch-wide slip of fabric with her fingertip. Light brown dust covered the rough, homespun material, as though someone had rubbed it in the dirt.

When Frederick dragged Samuel to the root cellar.

Dread clawed at her chest as she stared again at the dusty fabric and groped for a credible answer. Absolutely nothing came to mind other than the reason she was determined to deny: that Samuel's spirit was haunting her.

Could something as mundane as a piece of ribbon discredit everything she believed about life, death, and the nature of the universe?

Her first instinct was to pack her bags and head to Aunt Ginny's. But fleeing wouldn't help. She would still face a truth she wasn't ready to accept.

Shaking, she picked up the ribbon, tucked it into her back pocket, and went downstairs to find Nick...and return to the root cellar.

Chapter 12: Foul Play in the Root Cellar, Part 3

Nick eyed Bethany closely as he grasped the root cellar door handle. "Are you sure you're up for this? We don't have to go down there, you know."

"I'm fine. And of course I'm going down." She held his gaze. The eerie materialization of Samuel's hair ribbon had convinced her his remains were buried there. And she wouldn't get any rest until she found them. "We have a bet, and I'm not backing out."

He shot her a cautious grin. "If you're doing this, then I am, too. At least you'll be warm today." He lightly patted her shoulder, which was encased in his extra-large Maryland hoodie. The one she forgot to return yesterday. Her cheeks warmed at his touch.

He pulled the cellar door open. "Ready?"

Nick started down the steps, carrying a rechargeable lantern that illuminated the area much more effectively than the flashlights. Bethany surveyed the floor, her nerves on edge as she automatically rubbed the rear jeans pocket holding Samuel's black ribbon. The root cellar was no longer just a dank underground room. It was also Samuel's final resting place. His grave.

With a shudder, she kneeled and began clawing at the dirt with the hand rake. Beside her, Nick turned the soil. He was unusually quiet this morning. Did he really want to be here? Or had he accompanied her just to placate his aunt? In any event, Bethany was grateful for his help. She wanted to finish the search as soon as possible.

"I'm glad you brought the lantern," she said, dragging the hand rake through the soil. "But it's still creepy down here, even with the extra light."

"Yeah, but it doesn't bother me. I must be used to the ghoulish atmosphere that comes with these old places." Nick continued to sift through the soil as he spoke. "But if you start feeling weird...you know, lightheaded or headachy...then we need to leave."

"So far, I'm good. Getting used to the spookiness. And the whole idea of ghosts."

He faced her, and the space grew silent as his shovel hovered, motionless, over the dirt. "That's surprising. Coming from a staunch nonbeliever."

She considered showing him Samuel's hair tie but decided against it. Once she acknowledged her epiphany that yes, ghosts are real, there was no taking back her words. Instead, she would take her time, ease into that revelation.

"Well, there's a possibility you might be right."

He inched closer to her, his mouth relaxing into his familiar smirk. "Oh, I'm sure I'm right. About what, exactly?"

"About Samuel's spirit haunting the inn. I think I've sensed his presence in the kitchen. Like sudden cold spots, for example. And the faint scent of lavender."

He resumed sifting. "I've sensed those things, too, although I chalk up most of my experiences to the quirks of an old house. But some are really hard to explain away."

"I know." She stopped and peered at him. "Like the sensation that someone is touching you."

"You've experienced that?" He frowned.

"In the inn's kitchen. I felt someone's hands on my shoulder and heard Samuel's voice in my head. Like he was whispering in my ear."

Nick put down the shovel and straightened his glasses. "Jesus, Bethany. Why didn't you tell me this before?"

"Because I thought I was imagining it."

"What changed your mind?"

"Yesterday, I heard Samuel down here, too." She glanced at Nick, attempting to gauge his reaction, but his face was unreadable. "He told me he was wearing his signet ring, and finding it will lead us to him."

"That's what we're looking for? His ring?"

She nodded. "As much as I want to uncover it, part of me hopes we don't. Because it would prove he suffered a brutal death."

"When did he tell you about the ring?"

"Right before…" She hesitated, thinking of the best way to describe what had happened.

His brows drew down, and a crease formed between them. "Before what?"

She didn't expect the gravity in his tone, and grew wary. Maybe acknowledging her revised opinion on ghosts and hauntings was a mistake. But backing away now wasn't an option. She'd opened the gate and had to deal with the fallout.

"Before his impassioned reaction when I told you I was leaving the cellar. That's what gave me the headache. I felt his anguish inside my head."

Nick stared at her, his face falling into a scowl. "I wish you'd mentioned this sooner." He averted his eyes, running his fingers through his hair while processing her admission. "Aunt Margaret was right. We shouldn't have come back down here. It's not a good place for you, and we need to leave." He stood and started gathering their tools.

His response surprised her. If he reacted this strongly to Samuel's voice in her head, what would he do if he found out about the hair tie?

"Wait," she said, stopping his hand before he could grab her rake. "I'll be fine. Samuel's quest to uncover the truth compelled his spirit to reach out to me. That's all."

"Reach out?" Nick frowned as he clutched the backpack. "Bethany, he hurt you. That's not okay."

"He didn't mean to. I'm sure it won't be a problem going forward."

"I hope not. Because if it happens again, we're leaving for good. Period. I'll carry you out of here if I have to."

"Got it."

As she spoke, Bethany felt a brush of cold air swirl past her. The sensation was softer, calmer, and not as aggressive as the first time she'd felt it in the root cellar. And then she heard a light and comforting whisper. Samuel's voice. Not panicked this time, but smooth and assuring.

"I am deeply grateful to you, Miss Bethany. And to the gentleman assisting you. I won't hurt you again, trust me."

She peered at Nick. He'd retrieved his shovel and was again on his knees, sifting through the dirt. As if sensing her gaze, he looked up and sighed.

"That episode yesterday scared the hell out of me. I hope you're right about Samuel behaving himself, because nothing is worth putting you through that again."

"I am. Because Samuel has too much at stake to risk another outburst."

****

Outside the root cellar's entrance, Bethany stretched her shoulders as she and Nick sat side by side on the stone wall. They'd been raking and sifting for several hours and decided to take a break. The sweet scent of wild clematis was a welcome change from the cellar's dankness, and her body buzzed with warmth. She wasn't certain if the heat came from the midday October sun or the touch of Nick's knee against hers. Either way, she wasn't about to shift her position and risk a chill.

Today, Mrs. Snowden had packed ham-and-cheese sandwiches for them. Bethany pulled one out of a small cooler and handed it to Nick. He smiled, and she sensed his mood had lightened.

"Now that I'm open to the possibility that Samuel's buried down there, we should call off our bet," she said.

"What?" Nick held his sandwich in midair and winced. "That's not a reason. We bet on whether we'd find anything." He rubbed the stubble on his cheek with his free hand, stifling a smirk as he studied her. "The way I see it, there's two ways to approach this. You concede we'll find Samuel and buy me dinner now, or you wait and buy me dinner after we locate his remains."

"You're saying that either way, I'm on the hook for dinner?"

"Sounds fair to me." He laughed, a rich sound that resonated with warmth, and she couldn't help but smile in response. Time spent with him was restorative, healing.

"So," he continued, "this break you needed from

Oklahoma City. Was the reason job-related? Or did something else drive you to seek refuge in our little town?" He bit into his sandwich and watched her expectantly.

His question knocked her upbeat outlook down a notch. She'd barely thought about Owen the last few days. The anger and hurt from his affair had dwindled, leaving only a slight, imperceptible scar. Still, the broken engagement was part of her story, and she needed to tell Nick about it. This was her chance to tear off the bandage and air out the wound. But, for reasons she didn't know, Nick thought she was the type to love and leave. So bringing up the failed relationship in Oklahoma City that sent her fleeing to Worthington Cove filled her with apprehension.

She took a bite of her sandwich, stalling for time to think of a response. *I broke off my engagement to a man who cheated on me and then I came here to get away from his world so I could figure out a path forward without him.* But was this the right moment to explain everything? It might be better if she held off. Just for a little while.

Bethany finished chewing and swallowed. "I'm dealing with some personal issues, and this was the perfect place to get some time away. It's quiet. Familiar. And Aunt Ginny is here. She's always been my go-to person for moral support. Besides," she added, "I couldn't pass up a chance to see the renovations done on the old haunted mansion."

He chuckled. "Ah, so you *did* come here to hunt for ghosts."

"Believe it or not, ghostly encounters weren't on my agenda." With a laugh, she rolled her eyes. "But I've always been interested in my family heritage, and the Worthingtons who built Horatio House were my ancestors."

"Are you into genealogy? Like tracing your ancestry through DNA?"

"Not really. That's Aunt Ginny's thing. She's mapped something like nine generations of our family history." Bethany retrieved a cookie from one of Mrs. Snowden's containers. "I'd never want to do the work required to pull it all together, but the results are interesting."

"So you're related to Ariella on your mother's side?"

"Yep. Aunt Ginny confirmed we're direct descendants of Ariella and Samuel's daughter, Catherine. You might be, too."

He raised his brows. "Oh?"

"Catherine Watts married Benedict Dorsey. Is he one of your ancestors?"

"I have no idea. But it could explain why the Dorsey family inherited Horatio House."

"Aunt Ginny mentioned that your family owns it, as well as other things."

His eyes flashed impishly as his lips curved upward. "What other things?"

She shrugged. "That my mom's side of the family inherited Cornelius Day House. Aunt Ginny and my mom grew up there." *Plus it's haunted, and the ghost bothered my mom for years.*

"And here I was hoping you two talked about me." He playfully nudged Bethany's arm with his elbow. "Seriously, though. Did you tell her about our search in the root cellar?"

Her pulse quickened at his touch, so she took a deep breath to slow the rapid cadence of heartbeats echoing within her chest. "I did."

"And what was her reaction?"

"She wasn't happy about it and told me to be careful."

"Oh." Frowning, he avoided her gaze as he grabbed a water bottle. "Is she worried about you spending time with me?"

"Well, to be honest." Bethany looked down at the ground, trying to suppress a snicker. "She thinks you're, uh…a nice young man."

His expression eased into a smirk as he gave her a lighthearted shove. "You're in so much trouble. My heart almost stopped when I thought your aunt might not approve." He shifted toward her, wrapping his arms around her waist and pulling her body nearer to his until they were nose to nose. "And what about you?" He searched her face. "Do you think I'm a nice young man?"

"Maybe," she murmured.

"Well, I think you're a nice young woman." Nick brushed his lips against her cheek, nuzzling her skin until his mouth found hers. The touch of his lips, soft yet firm, unlocked need and desire so strong that her blood pounded.

Wriggling even closer, Bethany placed her arms around his neck and returned the kiss, capturing his lips with a passion that left her gasping for breath. His fingers caressed her cheek, then trailed along her chin and down her neck before dipping beneath the borrowed sweatshirt to explore her collarbone. The touch ignited a fire deep within her. She'd never felt such intensity with Owen, this yearning to hold on to someone so tightly, and she tensed, fearing the magnitude of her hunger and wary of losing control.

Am I ready for this? To be more than Nick's friend?

Teenage insecurity and twenty-something caution poked at her brain, reminding her of the pain Nick caused all those years ago. She grasped his hand to still his investigative fingers and pulled away, breathing deeply to calm her racing heart.

"We should go back down to the cellar. After all, we came here to search for Samuel's remains."

He nodded, his eyes smoldering as he lightly ran his finger across her jawline before dropping his hand. "Okay. Let's do this."

****

Although the cellar's gloomy dankness tamped down the blaze kindled by Nick's touch, the residual tingle distracted Bethany from the task at hand. She pushed herself to concentrate on finding Samuel's ring as she scrutinized the untouched portion of the dirt floor in front of her, but the effort lasted only a few minutes before she glanced sideways at Nick. A lock of dark hair dangled precariously over his forehead and snagged her attention. From there, her gaze moved downward to his nose, his cheeks, and finally his mouth.

Nick didn't seem to notice her watching him. He sifted through the loose soil like a man on a mission. What motivated him to keep probing the dirt? The work down here was undeniably tedious. Was it the challenge of uncovering Samuel's remains? Or could it be part of a plan to steer their friendship to the next level?

Her thoughts drifted to Owen as she raked. He and Nick were vastly different, almost to the point of being exact opposites. Owen was all about financial success, and he often tried to improve her, as though she wasn't up to par and needed guidance. He would consider this root cellar expedition to be an unproductive, time-wasting activity since it neither enhanced her resumé nor boosted her earning potential.

At one time, she would have agreed. But spending the last few days in Worthington Cove had altered her way of thinking. Her worth shouldn't be contingent on the amount of money she made or her ability to further her career. That's not how friendship—or love—worked.

She was pretty sure Nick shared this view. He was supportive and accepted her, even when they disagreed. Deep down, she knew he was scrabbling down here because he cared about her. And for him, that was reason enough.

As if finally sensing her gaze, he looked up and immediately formed his captivating, lopsided grin. "How's it going over there?"

"I'm slowing down."

"Me, too. How much longer do you want to keep working? We've been at it for a while now."

"Not long." Her body was getting stiff, and she was ready to stop. "I've been thinking about Dempsy's. I loved their ice cream growing up. Do they still make that brownie sundae?"

"Oh, yeah." He laughed. "And they still serve it in a humongous glass sundae dish. Just like they did when I was ten."

"Then I have a proposition for you." She straightened and flexed her back muscles. "I'll concede right now that you're the winner of our bet if you'll pick Dempsy's as your restaurant of choice."

"I don't know." A smile played on his lips as he feigned deep concentration. "I was going to hold out for someplace much, much fancier."

"If I recall, that sundae comes with three scoops of vanilla ice cream." She raised her brows and licked her lips. "And lots of hot fudge, along with a mountain of whipped cream and three cherries. Three! How can you say no to that?"

He let out an exaggerated sigh, then grinned. "I can't." Then, standing, he extended his hand to help her up. "I'm ready now."

"So am I. Shall we go?"

As they turned toward the steps, the air temperature dropped and the cellar door slammed. She looked at Nick. "I think the wind blew the door shut."

He bounded up the steps and pressed on the old wooden door with his palms. "Damn. It's stuck." She watched at the foot of the stairs as he aligned his body against it and pushed with his shoulder. The door didn't budge.

"What the hell?" he growled.

"You can't leave. Not yet."

The voice floated into Bethany's consciousness along with an iciness that slid down the core of her torso. Shivering, she crossed her arms over her chest and rubbed her biceps for warmth.

"Samuel?"

"Your search...it's incomplete."

"Samuel, please open the door."

Nick pushed on the door again, but it remained shut. She heard him mumble an expletive before loudly grumbling, "Seriously?"

"You're so close to discovering my remains. You

can't leave now."

Samuel's response, filled with urgency, filtered through Bethany's head and caused a dull throb to pluck at her temples.

"We've been at it all day," she groaned, struggling to keep her voice low. "We need a rest."

"Don't leave me here. I beg you!"

"We're not abandoning you. I promise. But we're done for the day." The throbbing escalated, and she rubbed the sides of her forehead, struggling to remain calm. "Please, don't fight me on this."

"But—"

Bethany's head pulsated, the dull ache sharpening into something more painful. "Samuel. You're hurting me. Open the door. *Now!*"

His answer was a release of frigid air that swirled near her face. Then she heard Nick call down the stone steps.

"Bethany, did you say something? Are you okay?"

"I'm fine. Try the door now."

A loud whack, followed by several unintelligible words, reverberated from the cellar's entrance. Bethany's anger surged.

"We had a deal, Samuel, and I trusted you to honor it." She pulled the dusty black ribbon out of her pocket and waved it. "Apparently, your honor is nonexistent and the hair tie means nothing."

A touch of warmth returned to the still air, and a fleeting sensation of remorse swirled through her skull as her pounding headache receded.

"I deserve your harsh words and I will strive to keep my word. My honor is important to me, Miss Bethany."

Bethany lifted her chin, acknowledging Samuel's

message, and shouted up to Nick. "It should be good now."

Two more wooden thuds echoed throughout the space, then Bethany heard a muffled, "Finally!" Daylight streamed through the entrance, and Nick appeared as a silhouette as he stood with his hand extended. She hurried up the crumbling steps.

"That was weird," he said, pulling her against him and heading toward the path.

"It was Samuel. He didn't want us to leave."

He stopped. "That was Samuel's doing? He wouldn't let me open the door?"

"I don't think he'll do it again. He said it was a mistake." She looked up and saw him frowning at her fingers.

"Bethany, what's in your hand?"

She flinched. It was time to tell Nick about the hair tie.

"It's a token. From Samuel."

His scowl deepened as he peered at the sliver of fabric. "From Samuel?" His voice was barely audible as he held out his hand. "Can I see it?"

"It's his hair tie." Her hand shook as she placed the dusty piece of cloth in his outstretched palm. "In my dream last night, Samuel took it off and fastened it around my wrist. He said it's a confirmation that he intends to manage his emotions so I don't suffer from any more of his outbursts."

Nick fingered the material in his palm.

"It was on my arm when I woke up this morning."

A parade of emotions flitted across his face. None of them were reassuring.

"And yes, it freaked me out," she added.

His mouth settled into a frown as he stared at the hair tie.

"I don't have any other explanation for how it got there. Except that Samuel actually tied it around my wrist. Which seems impossible, unless my interactions with Samuel aren't just dreams and his spirit really is haunting me." She sighed, wishing Nick would say something, anything, that would help her figure this out.

He lifted the ribbon closer and scrutinized it. "It's covered in dirt," he mumbled. "Like someone dragged it across the ground." He looked at her, his eyes questioning. "And you're sure you didn't find it yesterday while we were digging?" He squinted as he held the ribbon up to the sunlight. "Maybe you put it in your pocket and forgot about it."

How could he say that? She gaped at him, astounded. Now that she'd acknowledged Samuel's presence as more than a dream, he was the one who doubted Samuel actually gave her the hair tie?

"Of course, I'm sure," she huffed. "Even if I had found it here and taken it back with me—which I didn't—I couldn't have tied it around my wrist in my sleep."

With a snort, she grabbed the hair tie, stuffed it into her back pocket, and stepped away from him. "Apparently, it's not a problem to attribute cold spots and smells to a ghost. But linking the appearance of a tangible artifact to a spirit is unrealistic?"

Neither spoke for several minutes. Then Nick broke the silence.

"It's not that I don't believe you. It's just that I've never heard of anything like this before. A spirit transferring an object from one dimension to another.

And I'm…I don't know. Stunned."

He gently pulled her closer and wrapped his arms around her shoulders. "This ribbon? It takes your encounters with Samuel beyond intriguing to alarming. Especially since his presence has caused you pain. And…" He paused for a moment, as though considering his next words. "I can't help but worry about you."

She looked up to meet his gaze and detected concern rather than skepticism in his brown eyes, which softened her defenses. "I get it. Honestly, it was hard for me to comprehend at first. It still is. Seeing his hair tie around my wrist was surreal. But I'm okay, even though this whole ghost thing has me on edge."

Nick expelled a breath, and his face relaxed. "You and me both."

"Yeah. Admitting I saw a ghost and believed his story about a murder and cover-up because he gave me a dusty old ribbon, one that supposedly went with him to the grave…" She paused. "I feel like a crackpot. It's morbid. And if someone else told me this happened to them, I'd think they were a raving lunatic."

He grinned. "If you were anywhere else, I'd say yes, you *do* sound like a crazy person. But Horatio House has a history of strange, unexplainable things. Just because I've never known a spirit here to pass on a physical possession doesn't mean it's impossible."

Bethany smiled back, amazed at the turn of events that drew them even deeper into this ghost hunt. Was it meant to be, as Samuel thought? Had fate brought her and Nick together again to help Samuel's spirit find peace and give them another chance to be more than friends? Or was it merely a series of coincidences that had brought them to this juncture?

Either way, she would continue the search. Her heart ached for Samuel. She knew a lover's lies were as painful as being stabbed with a knife, and in Samuel's case, he was the victim of both. He had suffered in life, and was still suffering. She couldn't turn her back on him.

"Well, I don't know about you," she said, "but I've had enough ghostly interference for today. Are you ready to get out of here and have an ice cream sundae?"

"More than ready." He chuckled and grasped her hand. "The next time we come, we'll have to prop the door open. Apparently, wayward spirits can't always be trusted to behave, even when they promise they will."

"No kidding." She smiled and squeezed his fingers. "But that shouldn't be an issue much longer, because I think we're close to uncovering something."

Chapter 13: Ice Cream and Burgers at Dempsy's

Bethany stepped inside Dempsy's and stopped. A barrage of memories bombarded her as the ambiance of the old-fashioned soda fountain transported her back to her summer days here as a kid. Little had changed over the years. The tile floor still formed a black-and-white checkerboard, ceiling fans hummed overhead, and soda dispensers lined the back wall.

She turned to Nick. "I always came in here with Sarah. It was one of our hangouts." She scanned the long row of red vinyl swivel stools next to the glossy black countertop, then grinned. "Do you mind if we sit at the counter? Sarah and I always grabbed the stools when we could. They were perfect for twirling."

"Don't mind at all. I like the counter, too." He winked. "But my twirling days are long gone."

His eyes radiated a playful sparkle that warmed her entire body and lowered her defenses. It would be so easy to stay here in Worthington Cove and spend time with Nick. Be more than friends. Explore a relationship with him.

"Bethany?" Nick's hand exerted a light pressure on her lower back as his words broke into her thoughts. "Do you have a seat preference?"

Suddenly sheepish over her romantic reverie, she quickly led him to the two empty stools near the far end of the counter. "These two," she said, hoping he hadn't noticed her inflamed cheeks. "They were our favorite. When someone came in, Sarah and I could see who it was by glancing in that big mirror on the wall. No one could tell we were being nosy."

"Sounds like something you two would do."

He handed her a menu. A quick glance told her the food choices hadn't changed, either.

"Do you recommend anything? Besides the brownie ice cream sundae, that is?"

"Can't go wrong with the Double Dempsy burger," he said. "It's big, and definitely worth it."

"That's what I'm ordering first. And then the sundae."

Bethany tucked the menu back into its spot and swiveled to face Nick. Her knee brushed against his and a spark jolted her skin, which started a chain reaction of sensation. Her nerve endings flared and launched a swarm of flutters that pummeled her chest and sent waves of heat throughout her body. She felt like a teenager again, nervous and excited to be sitting next to her exceedingly handsome crush.

His lips curved into a smile as he watched her. "Me, too."

She gulped in air. Was he implying that his response to the unintentional touch was the same as hers? No way. He meant his food order. Still, the thought of his pulse soaring from her touch left her breathless.

"Then I know I made a good choice."

After the server took their order, Nick held her gaze for a long moment. His brown eyes were warm and engaging, and she couldn't look away.

"Did you know that the first time I saw you, you were sitting here at the counter with Sarah, consuming an entire brownie sundae? You were twirling and lost your pink flip-flop. It went flying across the room."

"The one with the giant orange flower. I remember that day." She laughed. "It was the first summer my parents went back to Oklahoma City and let me stay on with my grandparents. I was eleven, and the whole incident left me extremely embarrassed. It landed near an older boy. He was super cute, the kind that eleven-year-old girls swoon over. Of course, he saw the shoe and brought it…" She stopped and raised a brow. "Wait. Was that you?"

"Yep." His face lit up as he grinned. "I didn't recognize you, and I knew all the kids in town. So I asked around and found out you were Sarah's cousin, and Zach's cousin, too. But I didn't see you again until the next summer."

"Yeah, the summer Zach conceded that Martie and I weren't total dorks, and it was okay for us to be seen with him and his friends," she said. "When I met you, I didn't realize you were the flip-flop boy."

"That's because you wouldn't look at me when I gave it back."

"Because of utter mortification. I was hoping if I stared at the floor long enough, it would open up and swallow me. And you wouldn't discover the true identity of the stool-twirling, flip-flop flinger. Sarah didn't help matters, laughing as hard as she did."

Nick chuckled. "For the record, I never thought you were a dork and was very influential in Zach's opinion change that summer."

As they waited for their food, he asked her about Sarah. She gave him a quick update on her cousin's auditing job with a large accounting firm in Towson and her new apartment near the university. Then he responded with a follow-up on his cousin Vickie, who'd occasionally hung out with them and now worked as a bartender at Ridgely's Tavern.

While he spoke, Bethany's mind drifted back to the summers she'd spent in Worthington Cove. Nick had taught her how to swim in the bay and taken her sailing on the *Pipsqueak*. They'd ridden bikes around town, hiked through the woods, fished in the creeks, and eaten ice cream cones by the fountain in Ridgely Park. Nick always had time for her, even though she was a girl.

Then, during her last summer in Worthington Cove, their relationship changed. They still swam in the bay, sailed his tiny boat, and hiked through the woods, but Nick wasn't a kid anymore. He'd grown up, filled out, and went from nerdishly cute to breathtakingly handsome. And she fell head-over-heels in love with him. Although it was a summer crush, her emotions were very real. Especially the heartache of being ghosted after she returned to Oklahoma City.

She shifted her attention back to the present. The connection that had pulled them together years ago was still there. And, for her, it was growing stronger. Was she brave enough to go all-in and give him a second chance?

He felt like the same Nick, trying to pick up where they'd left off that summer like nothing had happened. But she wasn't the same Bethany, and a serious romantic relationship with him couldn't work until she knew what had prompted his silence back then.

And she needed to tell him about Owen.

Owen. He'd played the part of the perfect fiancé and fooled her. So much so that the discovery of his affair had pushed her into a hole loaded with distress and fury.

But she was climbing out. Finding a fresh path. She didn't miss Owen and barely thought about him or the engagement ring she'd yanked off her finger. That old hurt was fading as she spent more time with Nick.

Her stomach lurched with guilt over concealing her failed engagement. If she wanted honesty from Nick about that last summer they spent together, he deserved the same from her. No more procrastinating.

"Nick, there's something you need to know." She summoned the courage to continue. "It's about the personal issues that brought me to Worthington Cove."

He raised his brows, his brown eyes curious. "You can tell me anything."

As she opened her mouth to speak, the server brought two red plastic baskets loaded with burgers and fries. She relaxed and grinned, sidestepping her earlier comment by reaching for the burger in her basket.

"This looks fantastic."

He studied her. "It does. But you were about to tell me why you came to Worthington Cove."

She hesitated, her resolve wavering. *Tell him.*

"I found myself in a situation that was difficult to handle. I needed space to clear my head and think things through. So I came here." *Coward.*

His chin dipped in a slight nod. "Well, I'm glad you did."

Bethany detected a hint of disappointment in his voice. He picked up a French fry and changed the subject as if he sensed she was hedging and didn't want to pry. "You're sure shaking things up at Horatio House. Aunt Margaret's having a great time listening to your ghost stories. Probably the most intriguing thing she's experienced in years."

"It's easy to empathize with Samuel." She lifted the burger, took a bite, then swallowed. "I know how much it hurts to have your heart broken. When someone deceives you, it shakes you to the core. Makes you question everything you believed was the truth. Samuel deserves closure, and I want to help him with that."

Looking up, Bethany caught Nick's gaze in the mirror. His eyes were somber.

"Something happened in Oklahoma that caused you a tremendous amount of pain. That's why you came to Worthington Cove, isn't it?" He reached over and grasped her hand before she could reply. "If searching for Samuel's ring is part of your healing process, then I'm glad to help."

"It is." *More than you know.*

"Well, then, think of me as Nick Dorsey, ghost hunting collaborator and artifact extraction specialist." His lips twitched with amusement. "It's part of my charm, you know. Which reminds me. I'm available tomorrow afternoon if you want to go back to the root cellar. And if you need to talk things through, I'm a fantastic listener."

"I'd like that." She looked forward to Nick's company. His pleasant, easygoing way put her at ease. But was he someone she could trust? A man worthy of her love? She wouldn't know until she accepted him as he was now and not as the seventeen-year-old boy who'd ghosted her so many years ago.

"We still have a lot to sift through," she continued. "But maybe we'll get lucky and find something soon."

As Bethany grinned at Nick's mirror image, the familiar tinkle of the entrance bell sounded. She automatically shifted her attention to the doorway's reflection.

No. It can't be.

A sharp spasm seized her chest as an attractive, blond-haired man dressed in an expensive-looking navy suit entered the diner.

Dammit. Dammit. Dammit.

When his eyes found hers in the mirror, he smiled confidently and sauntered over. She gripped the edge of the counter, swallowing down the queasiness roiling her stomach, and braced for a confrontation. She wouldn't lose it. Not here.

Then, summoning the most dispassionate expression she could muster, Bethany waited to face the man approaching the counter where she sat with Nick.

****

"Beth!"

Her first impulse was to ignore him, but Owen stopped behind her and wrapped his arms around her shoulders.

She pushed against his arms, trying to escape his grip. How could he possibly think it was okay to show up here in Worthington Cove? *Her* town. *Her* space. And then embrace her like she belonged to him? He was the last person she wanted to see, and his hug ignited a surge of anger. She fought the urge to punch him and scowled at his reflection in the mirror instead.

"Owen, what are you doing here?"

He spun her stool around to face him, and clasped her hands. "Sweetheart, we need to talk."

"No." Bethany wriggled her fingers out of his grip, struggling to keep her composure. "I'm here with a good friend. We're having dinner."

Owen's brow puckered as he turned toward Nick.

"A friend?"

Nick stood and moved closer to her. She placed her hand on his forearm, inhaling to stay calm.

"Nick, this is—"

"I'm Beth's fiancé," Owen interrupted. He leaned down and brushed Bethany's lips with his.

Oh, no. He *did not* get to kiss her. Or claim her as his fiancée. Bristling with rage, she pulled back and shoved Owen with both hands. "The hell you are."

Nick stepped between them. "Bethany? What's going on?" he asked, his voice bewildered.

She peered at Nick. Worry, mixed with regret, stabbed at her gut. She shouldn't have kept the breakup with Owen to herself for so long. It reeked of deceit, and she felt like a hypocrite.

"Owen's my *ex*-fiancé. We are no longer engaged and never will be again."

"But that's why I came." Owen reached around Nick and attempted to recapture Bethany's hands. "To make things right between us."

With her fists clenched by her sides, Bethany glared at Owen. "That will never happen. You cheated on me. There's no recovering from that, so you may as well go back to Oklahoma."

"It wasn't my fault."

"How can you stand there and say—"

"Stop." Nick rested his hand on Bethany's shoulder, his face neutral and dark eyes unreadable as he studied her for a long moment. "I'd better go. Clearly, you two have issues to work out."

She watched, stunned, as Nick took out his wallet, dropped two twenties on the counter, and turned toward the door. Did he think she was still engaged to Owen?

Her first instinct was to run after him and explain everything. Convince him there was absolutely nothing left between her and Owen, that their relationship was a thing of the past. But her body stayed rooted to the stool as he left the diner, her mind going blank as panic set in.

Could she fix this?

Bethany turned back to Owen, her rage restrained only by her dismay over Nick's departure.

"How did you find me?"

"I know you, Beth." The corners of his mouth turned upward into a smug smile. "You always talk about Worthington Cove. Where else would you go?"

"You've wasted your time coming here. Our engagement is over, and I want you to leave."

"Don't say that. I want to get us back on track. Continue with our wedding plans."

"That's impossible." She folded her arms close to her body, remembering the pain and humiliation she'd felt when his affair came to light. "Your fling with Kayla destroyed any chance of us having a life together. Frankly, I should thank her. If it wasn't for her forgotten lingerie, I would never have learned the truth about you. That you're a cheater. She helped me dodge a bullet, and I'm grateful for that."

His light gray eyes fixed on her as he stepped closer. "I know I made a mistake, and I've regretted it every minute of every day. Please don't hate me."

Bethany searched his face, looking for a hint of remorse, but the confidence emanating from his smirk belied his words, and she knew. To Owen, his mistake was carelessness that led to getting caught, not that he'd taken up with another woman.

"I didn't end our engagement because I hate you,

Owen. You deceived me. You're a liar. Untrustworthy. And I won't marry someone I don't trust."

"But Kayla pursued *me*. She seduced *me*. I didn't realize what she was doing until it was too late. But it's over now. I ended my relationship with her." He moved, standing even closer to her. "More than anything, I want us to move past this. Have the wedding we've been planning. Spend our lives together. What can I do to make things right? Please, tell me."

Owen clutched her forearms and gently pulled her to her feet. Then he wrapped his arms around her shoulders and secured her against him. Chest against chest and cheek against cheek. She inhaled and breathed in his air. His cologne filled her nostrils. For an instant he was the Owen who had captured her heart, the man she had loved.

But that Owen was an illusion. She'd been so taken by his handsome face, alluring demeanor, and high-ranking real estate career that she had completely misjudged him, didn't see his true character. And now, the realization that she fell for him because of his looks, appeal, and large salary sent a shudder down her spine. Well, she wasn't that person anymore.

She pulled her arms free of his grip. "I loved you. Trusted you. And you tossed all of that aside when you slept with Kayla." She took a step toward the door, her voice firm as she spoke. "You can't talk your way out of this. I'm a stronger person now. No longer someone you can fool with your charm. And I'm done with you."

"We'll see, Bethany. I'm not giving up on us."

Ignoring his reply, she marched out of the cafe.

****

That night, Bethany lay in bed and stared at the

shadows cast by flames flickering in the fireplace. The dark gray shapes in the room produced a melancholy aura that matched her mood over Owen's sudden appearance at Dempsy's. She'd never imagined he would remember Worthington Cove, much less take a chance she was here and come searching for her.

Damn him!

Had he followed her here to restore his wounded pride? Or was it the challenge of reestablishing their engagement? She doubted it was love that motivated him. He hadn't even said he loved her! Only that he wanted to make things right. Whatever the reason, his coming here was pointless. He couldn't win her back. Now that she'd gotten to know Nick again these last few days, she realized Owen would never be the man she wanted. Ever. He should have stayed in Oklahoma City and continued his affair with Kayla.

She shut her eyes, attempting to block the tears that surfaced with the memory of Nick's expression just before he left the diner. Closed and unreachable. Whether it masked disillusionment, regret, or something else, she didn't know for sure. Only that his last words had sounded like a goodbye, and her fear that it was true left her numb.

"You're weeping. What's troubling you?"

Oh, great. Samuel's here. Bethany lifted an eyelid and saw him standing at the side of her bed, dressed in his usual attire. But his hair now hung loose and brushed the tops of his shoulders. His left hand rested on the iron frame of the headboard as he studied her with concern. She sat up, pulling the quilts close to her chin to ward off the chill that always occurred with his appearances.

"Owen. Why couldn't he have just stayed out of my

life?"

"Are you referring to the gentleman who accompanies you to the root cellar? The one with dark hair and spectacles?"

She shook her head. "No. That's Nick Dorsey. Owen is my ex-fiancé. I broke off our engagement and came to Worthington Cove. And now he's here, refusing to accept we're no longer a couple."

His brow creased as he sat on the edge of the mattress and faced her. "What caused this dissolution to come about?"

"I found out he was having an affair while we were planning our wedding."

"He was unfaithful?" His eyes narrowed. "This Owen fellow is assuredly unfit to receive your affections. Of course, you made the proper choice by ending the betrothal with such a loathsome rake."

"You're right. He's unworthy and I deserve better." She extracted her hand from beneath the blankets to swipe at her tears. "Still, I feel like an idiot. I spent the last five years of my life with him and never had a clue he was deceiving me until he got careless and I discovered his secret."

"A lover's infidelity causes great torment. It can be as painful as having your chest sliced open with a blade, if not more so." He scooted toward her, pulled a handkerchief from his trouser pocket, and tucked the square yellowed cloth into her hand. "Deception and loss of trust are hard to bear. I determined this to be true when I learned my dear wife may have hidden my son's true parentage from me."

After dabbing her cheeks, Bethany returned the handkerchief to Samuel and grasped his hand. "But you continued to love her despite your uncertainty."

"Like you, Miss Bethany, she was a beauty to behold. And yes, I'll love her until the end of my existence. With all of my being. But not only because of her exquisite features. She possessed a kind and caring disposition, as well as strength and determination." A somber smile touched his lips. "She was a force to be reckoned with, to be sure."

"I know you doubted she loved you, but I'm sure she did."

His hazel eyes grew moist as he surveyed the wall across from him. Bethany gently squeezed his icy fingers. "Our circumstances aren't the same, you know."

He turned his head toward her. "Hasn't each of us suffered the same type of anguish? Dishonesty regarding matters of the heart?"

"That part's true. But Frederick is the one who betrayed you, not Ariella. He was the one who came on to her, asked her to be with him, and speculated your son was his. She was an innocent bystander who had no intention of leaving you." She paused, focusing her thoughts. "And then Frederick put her in a terrible position. He took her husband's life—your life—in front of her. She must have been traumatized and heartbroken, walking around in a daze, trying to process her loss and barely registering what was going on."

"I suppose that's possible."

"When you think about it, she was also a victim. He betrayed her, too, when he murdered you. In one moment, she went from beloved wife to a widow responsible for the welfare of her children. What a horrendous burden he thrust upon her. Marrying him may have been her only chance for survival."

"Perhaps your version represents the truth," Samuel said, looking away.

"Of course it does. I'm sure Ariella's heart belonged to you, even if her family planned your marriage. That night, she pushed Frederick away. Told him she loved you and wouldn't leave with him."

Bethany released her grasp on his hand and wiped her eyes, willing herself not to tear up again. "But in my case, I don't think Owen ever really loved me. He felt no loyalty toward me or our relationship. He cared only for himself. At least I uncovered his true nature before I married him."

"You, Miss Bethany, are indeed the fortunate one." Samuel leaned in and gently brushed away the tears trickling down her cheek. "At the risk of overstepping, may I ask how you learned of Owen's unfaithfulness?"

"I found something in his room." Bethany hesitated, combing her mind for a term Samuel would understand. "An undergarment. Something a woman would only remove if she was undressing for…" Her cheeks burned as she continued, "…an intimate encounter."

His eyes grew wide with shock. Then, with a nod of understanding, he lifted her fingers and pressed them between his frigid palms before muttering, "Wretched cad."

She shivered, remembering the search for her shoes at his apartment and discovering a lacy red corset under the bed. Something she'd never owned. "I confronted him. Showed him what I'd found. At first, he denied that anything was going on. But I knew he was lying. Turns out, he was seeing a woman from his office. Kayla."

"This woman was under his employ?"

"No. A coworker. She's been with the company for

as long as I've known Owen. They were always very close. He told me they were just colleagues. But now I know otherwise."

"Why didn't he court her?" he asked.

"I wondered that, too. Kayla is a very ambitious person. Probably too much so for Owen. After thinking about it…a lot…I figured he didn't want to marry someone he thought might be better at his job than he is."

"So, he preferred her as a mistress rather than a wife." Samuel's brows narrowed and the edges of his lips turned downward. "If she was agreeable to that arrangement, most likely it would never change. And you…" He paused, his frown deepening. "Pardon my vulgarity, Miss Bethany, but you deserve a man who won't bring a whore with him to the marriage."

"That's exactly why we will *never* get back together." She looked down at her hand nestled within Samuel's. "Although he's pestering me to change my mind and return to Oklahoma. To marry him."

"I trust you will continue to be strong. And, rest assured, you'll find a suitable gentleman who will love you completely." His face brightened. "Perhaps you already have. The bespectacled man assisting you in the root cellar. Mr. Dorsey."

"Nick *is* pretty amazing." Despite the effort to be upbeat, her throat constricted. "When I told him your story about the knife fight with Frederick Howard, he suggested we sift through the root cellar to find your remains. I'm glad he did because I enjoy spending time with him. Our friendship was developing into something more. But now, because of Owen…"

Samuel leaned in, grimacing. "Good lord. What did that debaucher do?"

"Owen told Nick we're still engaged." A sob escaped her throat. "I hadn't told Nick about my broken engagement. I planned to explain the situation, but I waited too long, and now Nick is gone." She swiped at the tear cascading down her cheek. "He might have been the right guy for me, the one who would love me completely. But now, I'm sure he has doubts about me... probably thinks I'm deceitful and led him on."

"So this Owen character lied to Mr. Dorsey about your betrothal." Samuel's voice oozed disdain. "Why, that man is nothing more than a scoundrel. Undoubtedly, Mr. Dorsey will see that."

Would he? Bethany held Samuel's gaze and shrugged. She hoped he was right, but Nick had blindsided her before when he'd ended their relationship without an explanation. Was that his way of doing things? To cut and run before getting too invested? It would save *him* from heartache. But what about her? Maybe she was better off that Nick had stepped away. At least she'd avoid the anguish of being dumped when her heart was completely attached.

"I don't know. Nick disappeared once before without an explanation. It wouldn't surprise me if he did it again. I guess that's what he does."

His brow creased as he observed her, his tone unsympathetic when he spoke. "It appears you have already judged him."

"But isn't that what we do—you and me?"

He stood, glowering, and dropped her hand. "What do you mean? I most certainly do not judge men until I hear their declarations."

"But what about Ariella? Did you give her the chance to explain why she was there with Frederick

Howard that night? Or did you assume the worst and act on your assumptions?"

Cold air brushed her cheek as Samuel stared at her, his lips pressing together to form a tight line. "Howard was attempting to defile my wife's virtue. I witnessed his advances."

"You also heard her tell him she loved *you*, her husband. Maybe Frederick was giving her a farewell embrace. Did you ask him? Or did you just rush in with your knife out?"

His scowl deepened. "Is it your intention to provoke me?"

"I merely asked you a question. But your response tells me you didn't give either of them an opportunity to explain, that your jealousy took control and, because of it, you reacted with fury rather than thinking it through. And the price you paid was your life."

He recoiled, and a frigid gust slammed into Bethany, assaulting her skin beneath the quilts. The warmth seeped out of her body and she shuddered as Samuel glared at her in silence, his eyes dark and his mouth turned down.

She'd gone too far and for what? His spot-on observation that she was judging Nick prematurely? It was true. She couldn't deny it.

"I'm sorry," she said, facing his grimace. "My last comment was uncalled for. And hurtful. You're trying to be supportive, and what do I do? Lash out at you because I'm angry that Nick left me at Dempsy's with Owen."

His face relaxed. "I understand all too well how anger can influence our words and actions." He reached down and lightly touched her hand.

"It's too late for me to redress my wrongs, Miss

Bethany, and I am doomed to live with that truth throughout eternity. You, however, still have the chance to make amends with Mr. Dorsey. So, I beg you, don't take this bit of good fortune lightly. If he's an honorable man, acknowledge him as such. And trust him until he gives you a reason not to do so. Your happiness depends on it."

Chapter 14: The Trouble with Owen

Bethany glanced around the kitchen and saw Nick sitting at the table, nursing his morning coffee. As she slid into one of the wooden chairs, he looked over at her, his eyes guarded yet questioning, and her heart faltered.

"How was dinner at Dempsy's?" Mrs. Snowden asked.

"It was good until an acquaintance of mine from Oklahoma City stopped in." Bethany held Nick's gaze as she answered.

"Owen Harlington?"

Bethany's breath hitched as she focused on the innkeeper. "You know him?"

Mrs. Snowden peered at Nick, then Bethany. "He's a guest here. Checked in yesterday. Said he was looking for you."

Dammit, dammit, dammit.

Bethany glanced at Nick, needing to know everything between them was okay and hoping he'd confirm it with a lopsided grin. But his face remained impassive.

"Nick, I didn't know Owen was in Worthington Cove until he walked into Dempsy's last night. He never mentioned where he was staying, and I didn't ask."

He shrugged, his expression neutral. "No need to explain. You two were engaged, and he came to repair the relationship." He looked down at his phone, avoiding eye contact with her.

"He's your fiancé?" Mrs. Snowden asked.

"No," Bethany said, staring pointedly at Nick. "My relationship with Owen is over. Our issues are irreconcilable."

An awkward quiet enveloped the kitchen as Nick met her stare. She couldn't read his face, and last night's panic returned. Did he think she'd misled him? Or had he assumed the kiss they'd shared yesterday was insignificant? She had to reassure him that Owen was no longer a part of her life.

"Nick, I should have—"

"Mornin', Beth."

Owen, looking suave and handsome as always, stepped into the kitchen. His attire was upscale casual— khaki pants and a pullover sweater—and he exuded a polished, confident air. Before she could dodge him, he bent down, kissed her cheek, and slipped into the seat beside her. "What're we doing today?"

Her entire body tensed as she fumbled for an answer. Her "we" didn't include Owen. He was on his own.

"*I'm* running errands this morning, but I'm sure Mrs. Snowden can recommend some sightseeing activities for you." She forced a stiff smile, fighting the urge to snap at him.

"What a great idea," Mrs. Snowden said, shooting an anxious glance at Bethany. "I have several brochures. Let me—"

"Thanks," Owen broke in, "but I'll tag along with Beth. I know this town means a lot to her. She can show me all her favorite places." He flashed the innkeeper a charismatic grin. "No doubt they'll become my favorite places, too."

Bethany bristled at his words. Typical Owen. Performing the role of the charming, thoughtful fiancé, trying earnestly to weasel into everyone's good graces. To control her irritation, she inhaled a lungful of air and willed herself to stay calm and reply in a voice that was friendly but firm.

"Thanks for offering to join me, Owen, but there's no reason for you to tag along, since we aren't a couple anymore."

She glanced at Nick, hoping to catch his eye and make sure he knew she had no intention of spending time with Owen this morning. But Nick, scrutinizing his phone again, didn't look up.

"Then I'll join you as a friend," Owen replied.

Ugh. It was bad enough that Owen had tracked her down. But attempting to insert himself into her plans? That was crossing the line. As she struggled to maintain her composure, Bethany felt a slight chill, followed by icy fingertips resting on both of her shoulders. She relaxed, and her heart rate slowed. Then Samuel's voice seeped into her mind, his words filled with disdain.

"This man was your betrothed? The one with the mistress? Obviously, he's a smooth-talker. Shame on him for continuing his contrivance."

Bethany dipped her chin, agreeing with Samuel's observation, then redirected her attention to Owen. "No, thank you." She inhaled to suppress her fury. "I'm handling this morning's errands alone, and Nick is helping me with a personal project this afternoon."

She looked at Nick, silently pleading with him to back her up. She needed time with him to resolve any misunderstanding from yesterday's fiasco in Dempsy's.

But her heart sank when he looked up from his phone and shook his head.

"I'm sorry, Bethany, but I can't." He stood and walked his mug to the sink. "My boss changed my assignment. I'm driving down to Crisfield this morning to collect water samples. I'm not sure when I'll be back." He studied her. For a moment, his eyes were vulnerable, then a mask of indifference slid over his features.

Had Nick requested the reassignment to avoid her? As Bethany watched him walk out the kitchen door, a heated flush rushed up from her torso, causing her head to throb. And then, of course, Owen aggravated the situation by calling after Nick with that annoying, victorious edge in his voice she'd heard so many times. "Hey, man, that's okay. I'll help Beth this afternoon."

Every inch of her skin burned with outrage. What gave Owen the right to talk as though she needed him to look out for her? Returning to the root cellar with him in tow was *not* something she planned to do. Ever.

"No need, Owen. I'll handle it myself." She practically hissed the words. "You've done enough."

"Oh, don't be silly, sweetheart. You know it can't hurt to have me there." He flashed his perfect smile. "When you think about it, I'm actually doing you a favor."

Her fingers clenched into fists. A favor? What was it, exactly? Wrecking things with Nick? The longer she sat there, the more her frustration escalated. She knew Owen. Once he discovered what her "personal project" involved, he'd make an excuse to back out. And likely mock her while he was at it. Call it a fool's errand. A total waste of time.

"Don't let him upset you, Miss Bethany." Samuel's

voice.

She took a deep breath. "Trust me, Owen. You don't want to help. Nick and I are searching for something buried in the inn's root cellar, and it requires raking and sifting through dirt. I can't imagine that's something you'd want to do."

"You're searching a root cellar?" He narrowed his brows. "What are you looking for?"

"A signet ring. One that belonged to a man who lived here around two hundred and fifty years ago."

Owen's face lit up. "Is it valuable?"

Bethany shrugged. "I don't know the ring's commercial worth. It's a family heirloom and has sentimental value."

"And you're trying to find it *now*?" Owen eyed Bethany, one brow raised in surprise and his voice dismissive. "I'm sure that ring is long gone. You can't be the first treasure hunter to dig around down there. I guarantee that some other descendant discovered it years ago by following the same clues."

Despite her irritation, she grinned at the notion. Who else would have had any inkling that something lay hidden under the centuries-old layer of soil? Especially when the "clues" were the unsubstantiated recollections of a ghost.

"He's wrong! Don't succumb to his drivel, Miss Bethany. I beg you."

Samuel's voice, filled with exasperation, infiltrated her head again as a sharp burst of cold air, saturated with the distinct scents of pipe tobacco and lavender, swirled past the table. Its intensity surprised her.

"Why'd it get so cold in here?" Owen asked, rubbing his forearms.

Mrs. Snowden glanced at Bethany, mouthed *Samuel,* then replied, "These old houses are always drafty."

Bethany masked a smile. "Think what you will about Samuel's ring, Owen. But my gut tells me it's down there. And I intend to find it."

"Well, if that's how you want to spend your time, then I'm in. Besides, I can't let you go down into a root cellar by yourself. I'm not the kind of man who does that."

Bethany stifled a laugh. Owen hadn't changed a bit, always thinking about his own interests above everything else and spinning it to appear altruistic. Well, she'd never agree to reinstate their engagement. It was time to assert herself. Here. On her turf. Using her rules.

Owen would soon realize his efforts were futile.

"I'll consider your offer," she said. "But there's no guarantee I'll take you with me."

"Don't worry. I won't let that numbskull ruin our quest. I promise."

Wisps of frosty, scented air swirled once more, although less intense this time. She looked over at Mrs. Snowden, who again acknowledged the ghostly draft with a nod.

Samuel's presence was getting stronger and more frequent. Although it was comforting now, would that still hold true as she moved forward with the search for his remains?

****

Bethany left Horatio House as quickly as she could. Without a specific errand in mind, she walked along State Street to clear the frustration simmering within her. The brisk air and bright autumn sun simultaneously cooled and warmed her cheeks with each step, and gradually her pace slowed as her irritation eased. She looked up and saw the town library. Aunt Ginny was a good listener and should be at work by now, so she climbed the steps leading to the building's heavy wooden door.

Her footsteps echoed as she walked inside, breaking the stillness in the foyer. The mahogany desk stood unattended, and Aunt Ginny wasn't anywhere in sight. Neither was anyone else.

"Aunt Ginny?" she called out softly. "Are you here?"

"Bethany!" Her aunt's head poked out from one of the adjoining rooms. "My goodness, you're an early bird." Aunt Ginny's smile was warm and welcoming as she adjusted her glasses. "I was just thinking about you and your comments on our plans for the history festival. Hold on while I get us some coffee."

Aunt Ginny disappeared and returned with two full mugs. "There was a fresh pot in the break—" She scanned Bethany's face and frowned. "What's wrong, hon? You look like you have the weight of the world on your shoulders." She led them to a table in the next room. "It's quiet this morning. We can talk in here."

"Nick and I were having dinner at Dempsy's last night when Owen showed up and claimed to be my fiancé."

"Owen's here? In Worthington Cove?"

"The man refuses to accept that our relationship's over and is trying to push himself back into my life. I told Nick that Owen and I were no longer together, but he left us at the restaurant." Bethany swiped her eyes to dispel the unshed tears. "I should have told him about Owen sooner, but the timing never seemed right. And then Owen appeared, and it was too late."

"I take it you're interested in something more than friendship with Nick?"

"Maybe." Seeing Owen again emphasized how amazing Nick was. And she wanted to give a relationship with him a chance. "The connection we had that summer is still there, as though it's been days instead of years since we last saw each other. He's good company. Easy to be with. We have similar interests. And…"

Aunt Ginny leaned in. "And?"

"We kissed. And all the attraction I felt for him that summer came rushing back. But this time, our bond felt stronger. Deeper. It left me gasping, like nothing I'd experienced before. Not with Owen or anyone else."

"So, no second thoughts about ending things with Owen?"

Bethany shook her head. "Aunt Ginny, I'm not sure I ever really loved him. It was the excitement and prestige of being his fiancée that I loved. He made me feel special. And now I realize he didn't love me, either. He loved the idea of me. I was someone who fit his image of the perfect wife."

"Then it's time to tell your parents. They need to know the wedding is off, and the sooner, the better. Then you can pursue a relationship with Nick with a clear conscience."

"You're right. I'll let them know Owen and I broke up and there's no chance for reconciliation." Bethany faltered, biting her lower lip to keep her voice steady. "But I don't know if Nick is still interested. Since Owen showed up, he's…" She choked back a sob. "He's pulled back. This morning at the inn, he seemed…distant.

166

Nothing like the Nick I've been spending time with these last few days."

Aunt Ginny gave Bethany's hand another squeeze. "Don't worry, dear. Nick will come around. I bet he's falling for you just as hard as you are for him. So trust your instincts. He's a smart man, and Owen's nonsense won't alter his feelings for you."

"I hope so, but I still wonder if a serious relationship with him is even feasible. My life's in Oklahoma City, though I'm not thrilled about going back there. And I doubt Nick would ever leave Worthington Cove. He has roots here. And family."

Behind her glasses, Aunt Ginny's hazel eyes radiated kindness and support. "When it comes to love, we all face challenges that come with difficult choices. Although it's easier to stay rooted where we feel safe, it's worth venturing out of our comfort zone if it means we'll find happiness."

"What, exactly, are you telling me?"

Aunt Ginny gazed pointedly at Bethany. "That Oklahoma City is your comfort zone, the easy choice. But your happiness may lie beyond its borders."

"You mean I should move to Worthington Cove? For Nick?" She blinked back another bout of tears. "Oh, Aunt Ginny. I'm not sure he wants me here."

"Not for Nick, dear. Move here for *you*. Your roots and family are here, too."

Bethany stared at Aunt Ginny. Leave Oklahoma City? Give up her home and her job? Did she even possess the courage to do that? She breathed in, realizing Aunt Ginny was right. She'd built a comfort zone around Owen, but his affair with Kayla had blown it apart. Now she had to forge ahead and rebuild her world. Was that even possible to do in Oklahoma City?

The idea of a fresh start in Worthington Cove was appealing. She loved the town and everything it offered: sailing and swimming, the beach and the bay. Aunt Ginny was here. And Nick.

Still, the thought of walking away from her life in Oklahoma City—her career and her home—was terrifying. What if she couldn't find employment? Or worse, what if Nick didn't want to see her again? If she started over in Worthington Cove, going back to her old life would no longer be an option.

"I don't know if I'm ready to think about doing something so…life-changing. I wouldn't even know where to begin."

"You could live with me while you figure things out. I'd love to have you for as long as you want."

She smiled at her aunt. "That's very sweet of you, but I can't expect you to take care of me. I'd need to find a job."

Aunt Ginny nodded. "I have an idea about that. Remember when I said we need a manager for our history festival? Well, you're a perfect fit! I shared your comments on the packet with the planning committee, and everyone agreed your input was just what we needed. You really know your stuff. And not just about lining up sponsorships. Your thoughts on the budget, scheduling, and recruiting volunteers are superb."

"Going through your planning documents was fun. I'm glad my input was helpful."

"It was. Very much so. When the town council members see your notes, they'll realize the planning committee needs professional guidance if they want the festival to be a success. I'm certain they'll approve the manager's position right away. And you're the person we need to make it all work."

Bethany considered her aunt's words. Organizing a town festival from scratch was an enormous project, but one that Bethany knew she could handle. And putting together that type of event sounded appealing. Still, she was uncertain it was the right choice. She'd worked hard to become the institute's development director, although the role itself had become routine and automatic. She'd stayed on because Owen had encouraged it. He'd said the prestigious title would help both of their careers. Even though her duties were no longer inspiring, she had enjoyed the esteem that came with the position. But was it enough to sustain a fulfilling future in Oklahoma City?

"It's just something to think about, hon." Aunt Ginny flashed her an enthusiastic smile. "Oh, that reminds me… I also sent your notes to Henry, the town council chair, and he asked if you would come to their meeting tomorrow night and present your ideas to the members. They might have questions, and you'd do a much better job answering them than Henry or me."

"Of course I'll go."

"Perfect! In the meantime, you're welcome to stay in my guest room if you're uneasy at the inn with Owen there. It'd give you a chance to sort things out without him hovering over you and trying to weaken your resolve."

As much as she wanted to avoid Owen, Bethany couldn't leave Horatio House. Not yet. She was committed to finding Samuel and didn't want to sever her connection with him.

"I appreciate your offer, but I need to stay at the inn. There's a strong possibility that Samuel's remains are in the root cellar, and I want to continue searching for them."

"Wait. What? You're going down to the root cellar again?" Aunt Ginny scowled and pushed on the bridge of her glasses. "I thought you didn't believe Samuel was buried down there. What changed your mind?"

It was time she told Aunt Ginny about the hair tie. Bethany pulled the dusty black ribbon out of her pocket and placed it on the table in front of her aunt. "This did."

Aunt Ginny frowned. "What is that?"

"Samuel's hair tie. I dreamed he gave it to me. And when I woke up the next morning, it was tied around my wrist."

Aunt Ginny stared at the slender piece of fabric for a long minute, then looked up, clearly worried. "Oh. How very…odd."

"Nick thought so, too." Bethany chuckled humorlessly. "And believe it or not, *I* convinced *him* it was a paranormal phenomenon."

Aunt Ginny reached out and rubbed her index finger over the slip of fabric. "I suppose your paranormal explanation *could* be true. It just seems so…"

"Unbelievable?" Bethany toyed with her coffee mug. "I've also experienced other unusual things in the house and root cellar."

Aunt Ginny raised her eyebrows. "Such as?"

Bethany shared everything: hearing Samuel's voice, sensing his touch in the kitchen, and his attempt to keep her and Nick from leaving the root cellar. As Bethany spoke, Aunt Ginny listened quietly, her expression shifting from uncomfortable to troubled before she removed her glasses and rubbed her eyes.

"Please stay at my house. The idea of you remaining

at the inn or going to the root cellar worries me."

"Really, I'll be fine. I don't sense any anger or malice from Samuel. The man is grief-stricken more than anything else."

"At least Nick will be with you."

Bethany sucked in a breath and released it. "Nick's not here. He took a work assignment in Crisfield and doesn't know when he'll be back." Tears formed as she pictured Nick's impassive face. Was his disappearing act a repeat of that summer? She swiped her cheeks and sighed. "Of course, Owen invited himself to the root cellar to help me. But the last thing I want is to spend time with that man."

Aunt Ginny stood and pulled Bethany into a hug. "Oh, honey. I'm certain everything's going to work out with Nick." She loosened her grip and faced Bethany, her eyes questioning. "Would it be so terrible if Owen helped you, since Nick's out of town?"

"I don't want to give Owen the wrong idea. He'll take it as a sign that we're engaged again."

"I'd breathe easier if someone is with you. Even if it's Owen. It would give you a chance to talk things out and help him accept the engagement is over and there's no way to repair your relationship. You never know, he may actually help with digging."

Bethany stifled a groan. Although she hated the idea, Aunt Ginny was right. It'd be an opportunity to end things with Owen for good. She could handle a couple of hours in the root cellar with him. And they might even make some progress in the search.

"I guess I could take him," she replied.

Aunt Ginny gave her another squeeze. "Thank you. I'll rest easier knowing you're not alone."

Chapter 15: Foul Play in the Root Cellar, Part 4

On her way back to Horatio House, Bethany stopped at Lindy's deli and picked up a crab cake sandwich and French fries for lunch. When she entered the inn's kitchen, Owen was sitting at the kitchen table with Mrs. Snowden. He stood, his gray eyes appraising as he stepped toward her. But she maneuvered out of his reach and slid into a chair. A hug was out of the question. Their relationship was over, and he needed to accept that.

She wished Nick was sitting across from her, grinning and planning another outing. But the image that pushed into her thoughts was his expression this morning—closed and distant. It lodged in her chest and settled there, like a heavy stone pressing against her sternum. She fought back a tear and retrieved the sandwich, unaware that Owen was behind her. He slipped his fingers beneath the neckline of her shirt and began massaging her shoulders. A flush heated her face. The gesture was far too intimate, and she angrily pushed him away, hating that her body still reacted to his touch when her mind was determined to move on.

"What the hell, Owen?"

"You seemed tense."

He rested his hand on her shoulder, and a cold blast of lavender-scented air settled around them. A low hiss buzzed in her ear. Samuel was there.

Owen stepped back with a shudder. "These damned

old houses and their frigid drafts make me feel like I've walked over someone's grave."

"It must be a sign, Owen." A smirk played on Bethany's lips as she glanced at Mrs. Snowden. "You're agitating the dead."

"Hilarious," he said, returning to his chair. "It almost sounds like you think the inn's haunted."

"I understand it's a possibility. Horatio House *does* have a reputation for that, you know."

With a laugh, Owen turned to the innkeeper. "Can you believe she actually said that? Sounds like Beth believes in ghosts." His voice held a tinge of mockery.

Mrs. Snowden raised an eyebrow. "The idea isn't as far-fetched as you—"

"Wait," he interrupted. "You can't possibly believe ghosts haunt the inn."

"I haven't ruled out the possibility."

The temperature in the room dropped and an icy prickle grazed Bethany's shoulder, causing a shiver to surge through her. Across from her, Owen scowled and rubbed his arms.

"Damn this cold air. Margaret, why is it so chilly in here?"

"It could be the ghosts." Mrs. Snowden grinned at Bethany, then walked over to the coffeemaker and refilled her mug. "After all, this place is over two hundred and fifty years old and has witnessed more than its share of tragedy. Many troubled spirits may still be here, roaming the house and the entire property."

"Like the root cellar," Bethany added, unwrapping her sandwich. "I wouldn't be surprised if you encountered a cold draft down there, too. Are you sure you want to go?"

"Of course I'm going." Owen studied her, his face smug. "I'm a grown man, for god's sake. You can't deter me with your silly ghost talk. I'd never take such nonsense seriously." He stood and caressed her shoulders again. "I'm surprised you'd even try. But I'll admit, the attempt was adorable."

She flinched at his touch. "Owen, don't—"

He leaned down until his cheek was next to hers. "But I want to help. Isn't that what you always wanted? To have shared interests?"

She leaned away, recoiling at the scent of his cologne—the fragrance of heartache and betrayal—as memories of their life together plugged her throat. She needed to stay strong, to remember he was a cheat and a liar.

"Don't worry, Miss Bethany." A tendril of wintry air swirled past her ear. *"Since that man is determined to accompany you to the root cellar, perhaps you should allow him to do so. I won't leave you with him unattended."*

Another draft touched her cheek.

"In fact, I rather look forward to joining you. He may need to be enlightened."

As much as she wanted to avoid Owen, taking him down to the root cellar might be the right call. Especially if an "enlightenment" convinced him to leave her alone. She stood and, with her arms crossed over her chest, scrutinized him.

"Okay, I'll take you with me. But this doesn't mean our engagement is back on. It's not. This is a chance for us to find closure, not reconciliation. Do you understand?"

"Beth…"

"That's what I'm offering. Take it or leave it."

She watched with satisfaction as a frown replaced his smug grin. "Fine. I'll take it."

****

The old wooden door wasn't as heavy as Bethany expected when she pulled it open and stared down into the blackness. Yesterday, in their rush to get out, she and Nick had left the lanterns on the dirt floor, so she aimed her phone's flashlight on the crumbling stairway to light the way down.

Owen peered into the dimness and wrinkled his nose. "You really want to go down there? I can smell the rankness from here."

Without answering, Bethany carefully navigated the stone steps. When her foot touched the dirt floor, the earthiness of the small room felt familiar, almost inviting. But the sentiment quickly dissipated when Owen reached the bottom of the steps and said, "God, it's so dark. Aren't there any lights down here? How are we supposed to find a ring?"

"Don't worry, I've got this."

With a sigh, she turned on the lanterns and studied the overturned soil. Although she and Nick had completed a sizable section, a large portion of the second plot remained untouched.

"One of us can rake the soil loose, and the other can turn over the loosened dirt and sift through it," she said, facing him. "Do you want to rake or sift?"

Owen looked around the cellar, frowning. "It doesn't matter. I'll do whatever that other guy did."

"Nick sifted." She pointed to a pile of soil and the small shovel. "You can see where we left off yesterday."

Bethany kneeled and began hacking at the dirt.

Owen moved to Nick's spot, except he checked his phone instead of picking up the hand trowel. When he finally started sifting through the soil, he commented on the absurdity of the venture and the time they were wasting.

She missed Nick and the serenity that blanketed her when he was near. His familiarity with her movements had enabled them to synchronize their tasks—dig, sift, dig, sift. And their easy banter, tossed back and forth as they worked, helped ease the monotony of the job. He incorporated fun into the search and brought joy to her life, emotions she hadn't felt with Owen or even realized were missing in their relationship. Until now.

How had she ever thought Owen was the right man for her?

Despite Owen's gripes, the swath of overturned dirt was growing. When the sifted portion had increased by about a foot, he put down the trowel, stood, and stretched his arms.

"Beth, this is pointless. We've been down here for an eternity and have nothing to show for it." He paced, poking the piles of soil with his toe before stopping to hover over her. "It's not like you to go on a wild-goose chase. What makes you so sure the ring is down here?"

"I discovered a family secret since I've been in Worthington Cove." She continued raking. "A murder."

"What does the ring have to do with it?"

"It belonged to Samuel Watts. He was the murder victim."

"Hold on. Are you talking about that guy who lived here around two hundred years ago?"

"Two hundred and fifty years ago. But yes, him." She stopped hacking at the dirt and looked up. "The historical records list him as being lost at sea. But that story was a cover-up. His killer murdered him inside Horatio House, then hid his body in this root cellar. He was wearing the ring when it happened."

Owen studied her. "If all the records said he was lost at sea, what makes you think someone murdered him? And then concealed it?"

"Samuel's spirit revealed the information. If I can, I'd like to help it find peace."

"His spirit? Like he's a ghost?" Owen gaped at her. "You're kidding me, right? That's a joke."

Bethany turned away to avoid his stare and resumed raking. "Samuel's rival stabbed him and dragged him down here to die. And his spirit has been…and still is…tormented by the experience."

"You're serious." Owen shook his head, frowning. "Holy shit, Beth. That's ridiculous. Have you lost your mind?"

The air got colder, condensing their breath to wisps of fog. A chill passed through Bethany.

Samuel was down here with them.

"Samuel trusted his murderer and paid for that mistake with his life. He wants the truth to be known." She looked up at Owen, her gaze steady. "I know how it feels when someone betrays you. It's painful, and hard to get over. But you haven't experienced that, have you? The shock and heartache of being deceived."

"C'mon, Beth." His voice was soft as he crouched down and lightly stroked her hair. "That's in the past. I wish you'd let it go." He cupped her chin with his hand and turned her head toward his. "I need you, and you know you need me. It's time to put an end to this bogus treasure hunt and get out of here." He leaned in and touched his nose to hers. "Let's go home."

"No." She twisted away, bristling at his touch. "I'm not leaving, Owen."

"Then the ring is worth a lot of money."

"Really? That's what you think?" She turned back to the plot, shaking her head as she hacked at the dirt. "It's evidence. Finding the ring will prove Samuel didn't drown in the Chesapeake Bay. That's the whole point of the search, Owen."

"I don't get it. Why do you care about some guy who's been dead for over two hundred years? That's a couple of centuries, Beth. Centuries! He'd be dead by now, anyway."

Why did she care? Was it merely to right a wrong, or did something deeper motivate her? She understood Samuel's distress. While she had the chance to overcome her grief and find someone worthy of her love, his brutal death had eliminated any opportunity for him to work things out with Ariella. To achieve closure.

"He's suffering, and I—"

"Beth, don't." He stood and glared at her. "Your time is better spent on the living. On us. You need to get over this ridiculous search and move on. It's time to go back to Oklahoma City and continue with our wedding plans."

She stared up at him, rage squeezing her lungs and making it difficult to breathe. He'd pushed her too far and needed to comprehend that he no longer had any influence over her. She inhaled deeply, dropped the hand rake, and stood to confront him.

"Owen, I'm *not* marrying you! It's over between us, and you have to accept it."

Frosty air touched her cheek, transforming her

breath into a cloud, and she heard Samuel's now-familiar voice seep into her thoughts.

"I'm here for you, Miss Bethany."

"Don't be angry, sweetheart." Owen stepped closer to her and ran his finger along her cheek. "We don't have to go home yet. We can hang around a few more days. But let's take a break from the root cellar. Go for a cocktail. Have a nice dinner while we're at it."

"No." She swiped his hand away, determined to stand her ground. "Although I appreciate your help today, I'm not having dinner with you."

"But you need to rest." His voice was low and wheedling. "We've spent the entire afternoon down here."

"I'd rather stay and get a bit more raking done. You can have dinner without me."

"No, Beth." Owen's voice reverberated through the cellar.

The force of his words shocked her, and she backed away. "Owen, I—"

"You left town to punish me. I get that. And I've done my penance. But enough is enough. It's time for you to come home."

The icy weight of Samuel's hands rested on her shoulders as his voice entered her thoughts.

"This fool is no match for you. You are my descendant. A Watts. My strength and the strength of your ancestors rushes through your veins. Tell him to be gone."

Samuel emphasized the word "Watts" with a sense of pride in his tone, and the strength in his voice reinforced her resolve. Yes, she was strong. Owen was no match for her. Not anymore.

Bethany squared her shoulders and took a step closer to him. "I told you our relationship is over, but you refused to listen to me. So let me tell you again. I'm not having a drink with you. Or dinner. We are no longer a couple. We are not engaged. And we are not getting married. We are done. You need to go back to Oklahoma. Alone."

Owen stared at her, his jaw flexing as his teeth clenched behind pursed lips.

"You want to give up a life with me for this? Combing through a dirt hole in a little crappy-ass town for some dead guy's ring? No, Beth. I can't let you do that."

Defiantly, she held his gaze, refusing to let him manipulate her. She deserved someone better than him. Someone who respected her for who she was. Like Nick.

She deserved Nick.

"We can go back and forth on this, Owen. But the truth is… You're not good enough for me."

Owen's hands tightened into fists as he glared at her. When he spoke, his voice simmered with controlled anger.

"I've dedicated the last five years of my life to you. Treated you like a princess. And now you tell me I'm not good enough for you?" He grabbed her upper arm, his eyes dark with rage, and pulled her toward him. "Oh, hell, no! I was good enough when you accepted my engagement ring and made a commitment to me. You're mine. And you're not backing out now."

Stunned, Bethany struggled to break his hold. "Owen, you're hurting me. Let go."

"Like you're not hurting me?"

As she worked to free herself from Owen's grasp,

an explosion of wintry air blanketed the cellar. In the biting cold, her body shook as puffs of dense fog escaped her lips.

Samuel. His presence had never been this strong. Then she heard him.

"Unhand her, you brute!" His voice was thunderous and commanding. Nothing like his whispers in her thoughts.

"Who said that?" Owen immediately released her arm, his face pale in the dimness.

Bethany blinked in surprise. Owen heard him, too?

"Samuel Watts," she replied, rattled by the intensity of Samuel's energy and questioning his ability to control it.

"Who the hell is he?"

"The man whose ring we're searching for."

"You don't mean the dead guy?" Owen scoffed. "Really, Beth! I don't know how you did that voice thing, but you need to drop the ghost nonsense. It's getting old."

"I told you I'm helping Samuel's spirit find peace. Obviously, he wants me to continue."

"That's bullshit." Owen seized Bethany's forearm and pressed his fingers into her flesh. "I'm not buying whatever hoax you're selling. Do you think I'm an idiot?"

"Take your hand off of me. I am not your property." Anger and alarm flared inside her chest. She'd never seen this side of Owen, and it was frightening. She tried freeing herself from his grip, without success.

Then Samuel's voice, intense and threatening, once again filled the root cellar.

"You ignored my request, you barbaric savage.

Therefore, I have no recourse but to escort you to the exit."

Another burst of freezing air filled the space, numbing Bethany's nose and lips. Owen's mouth opened and released a billowy cloud. He peered at her with confusion as he released his grip.

"Something grabbed my arm, Beth!"

"Sir, it's time for you to take your leave." Despite the civility of his words, Samuel's voice radiated fury.

Cold air rushed past her as it propelled Owen toward the steps.

"Oh, shit, now it's pulling me!" Owen shouted. "What's happening?"

Bethany stared at Owen, stunned. Samuel's power was escalating.

"Samuel! What are you doing?"

"This man is no gentlemen and doesn't deserve your compassion." Samuel's loud, angry tone reverberated throughout the cellar. "You asked him to leave, and he didn't comply. Instead, this…wretch…put his hand on you, intending to force you to leave with him. How dare he touch you!"

"Oh, god, make it stop!" Owen's voice, laced with panic, ricocheted off the stone walls.

Astonished, Bethany watched as an invisible force hauled Owen backward up the cellar stairs. His legs sagged as though he were a rag doll being dragged behind a child. She ran after him as the unseen hand continued to hoist him upward, oblivious to his cries of pain as his body repeatedly slammed into the hewn stone's sharp edges.

Owen caught her gaze, his eyes wild as they sent her a plea for help.

"Samuel," she cried out. "You need to stop!"

The air circled faster. "He had no right to force himself on you."

"You're hurting him."

"But he hurt you, Ariella! He's no better than a common bully. I must avenge your honor."

Ariella? Oh, god, is Samuel reliving the night of his murder?

Bethany rushed forward, concerned that Samuel's anger had pushed him too far and Owen might be seriously injured.

"Samuel, please listen to me! I'm Bethany, not Ariella. And he's not Frederick Howard."

The air calmed slightly as the force towing Owen paused at the cellar's opening, then Samuel's voice penetrated her thoughts.

"Bethany?"

"Samuel, you have to let go of him now. Before you do something terrible that you'll regret for the rest of your existence."

"Oh, my god. What have I done?"

She hurried up the stairs as Owen disappeared through the entrance, emerging in the sunlight in time to see him released into a pile of yellow leaves. As he stood and brushed the debris from his clothes, Bethany detected so much hostility in his stance that she took a step backward.

"Owen, are you okay?"

"What the hell was that, Bethany?"

"I told you. Samuel's spirit haunts the—"

"Just stop," he interrupted. "I don't know how you managed that trick, and I really don't care. You've gone way too far with your crazy ghost crap. And I'm done.

With this stupid search. Our relationship. Everything." His lips pressed into a sullen grimace. "I came here to give you another chance. To smooth things between us and get our wedding back on track."

Seriously? She stared at him, dumbfounded. "*You* were giving *me* another chance?"

"I was. But now…" He shrugged and shook his head. "I don't even know who you are anymore."

"Owen—"

"There's nothing you can say that will change my mind." He combed his fingers through his hair and straightened his sweater. "This new *you* is not someone I want to marry. The wedding is off."

Without waiting for her to respond, Owen turned and disappeared into the woods.

Chapter 16: Lost—and Found

Bethany sat on the flat rock near the cellar door, her cheeks turned toward the afternoon sun. She rubbed her arms, trying to dispel the chill that still gripped her. The last few minutes in the root cellar had played out like a weird, darkly lit horror movie. Except her experience wasn't some eerie, make-believe story. It actually happened. And it rattled her—not only Owen's attempt to control her, but Samuel's response.

Especially Samuel's response. His intensity was startling, but effective. Owen was no longer a problem.

She inhaled the autumn air, relieved that Owen had given up on his quest for reconciliation. Now that he was likely on a plane heading back to Oklahoma City, she felt lighter. Happier. Ready to move forward with Nick.

In the stillness, she heard the faint gurgle of water. Reluctant to go back to the root cellar, and unwilling to risk an encounter with Owen at Horatio House, Bethany ventured farther into the woods in search of the nearby stream. Rust, auburn, and golden foliage stretched in front of her as she wandered along a narrow, overgrown path, taking in the colors of fall. Her thoughts centered on Nick—the unmanageable bit of hair he always pushed off his forehead, the lopsided curve of his grin, and the way the skin around his dark eyes crinkled when he laughed. And apprehension seized her chest.

Where did she stand with Nick? Was continuing this

thing between them—whatever it was—even an option? Or had her hesitation to mention the failed engagement destroyed any chance for something wonderful with him?

Although they'd only recently reconnected, the extent of her affection for him was startling. While his sense of humor and easy smile had hooked her teenage heart years ago, it was his kindness and compassion that captivated her now.

The only way to move forward was to let go of the parts of her life holding her back and be open to new opportunities. Like a relationship with Nick Dorsey.

She spotted the stream and sat near the bank, propping her back against a large tree. Slender branches and fallen leaves floated past, captured by the gentle current, and her eyelids fluttered shut as her mind drifted along with the debris.

It was time to release the hurt of being ghosted and give Nick a chance to explain what happened. And she needed to assure him her relationship with Owen was over, with no chance of reconciliation.

Because she wasn't about to let the opportunity to be with Nick pass her by.

****

A crow cawed overhead, and Bethany sat upright with a start. Had she fallen asleep? The afternoon sun hovered much lower in the sky and more shadow than light filled the space around the trees. She checked the time on her phone. Five thirty. It'd been more than three hours since Owen headed back to the inn. Surely he'd checked out by now. She entered Horatio House's address into her phone and studied the blue dot on the map grid that marked her location. The stream was east of the house and the return hike should be easy with the phone to guide her.

She scanned the thicket and saw several trails winding through the trees. All were narrow and overgrown, and she didn't know which one had brought her here. No problem. The map would steer her in the right direction, no matter which path she followed. But when she tapped on the phone again, it didn't respond. She tried once more, and nothing. The battery was dead.

Anxiety clutched her chest as she poked at the useless screen. She had no desire to be stranded in the woods at night, and standing here wouldn't get her back. She had to pick a trail and move forward before full-on darkness took over the last bit of light. All she had to do was walk west, toward the sun, and the nearest path was as good as any other. But when she took a step, a stray vine caught her toe, and she tumbled into a clump of underbrush.

"Dammit."

As soon as the word escaped her lips, Bethany heard a branch snap nearby, followed by the crunch of dead leaves. Would someone be hiking out here this time of day? Or was it something else? She froze, wishing she knew more about the wild animals inhabiting these woods. Then, while scanning the trees, she detected movement in the shadows. She held her breath, hoping that whatever was out there would move on.

But it didn't. Instead, she saw someone coming toward her through the dimness, their footsteps quickly smashing through the vegetation as they approached. Her heart raced as she grabbed a nearby stick and braced herself for the encounter.

A moment later, Nick emerged from the thicket.

"Bethany!" he called out, rushing toward her. "Thank god!"

"Nick!" She scrambled to her feet, filled with relief. "I thought you were in Crisfield."

He gathered her into his arms, drawing her to his chest and holding on tightly. "Aunt Margaret called me. She said you took Owen to the root cellar and he came back to the inn alone. He was pretty upset when he returned and went straight to his room without saying much, then packed up and left. When you didn't show up, she panicked." He exhaled. "I was worried, too. So I came back to find you."

She savored the warmth of his embrace and, in response, wrapped her arms around his waist and snuggled up against him. She felt safe—cherished, even—and looked up, waiting for him to brush his lips against hers and let her know everything between them was okay.

Instead, he released her. "What are you doing way out here?"

Was he only worried about her as Mrs. Snowden's guest, and nothing more? She swallowed, her throat thick with disappointment. "I needed to process some things, so I hiked to the stream. It was so peaceful out here that I fell asleep. When I woke up, I was going to use the map on my phone, but it died and I wasn't sure how to get back to the inn."

"I need to let Aunt Margaret know I found you." He typed into his phone, then turned his attention back to her. "Are you all right?"

"I'm fine."

She took a deep breath. This was her chance to explain everything and clear up any misunderstanding about her broken engagement.

"Nick, Owen is not and will never be the person I want to spend my life with. I'm sorry I didn't tell you about our engagement and breakup."

"You can tell me now."

He held her gaze, his brown eyes intense as he sat down by a tree and motioned for her to sit next to him. She settled in and shared everything there was to say about Owen: their engagement, his affair, and the breakup.

"Owen has finally accepted I'm no longer his fiancée. And there's a good possibility he believes in ghosts now, too."

A smile touched his lips. "Sounds like you have a good story."

"Oh, I do." She laughed, then described Owen's departure from the root cellar.

"I wish you'd been there to see the look on Owen's face," she continued. "Fear-induced astonishment. Or maybe it was pure, unadulterated fright. Anyway, he broke off our engagement."

"Even though you'd already ended it?" With a chuckle, he reached over and clasped her hand. Her heart pounded at his touch. Was this a sign that he still wanted something beyond friendship?

"He just refused to accept it was over between us and kept insisting I go back to Oklahoma with him. That's what provoked Samuel. For a moment, I thought he might really hurt Owen. Or worse." She snorted. "It's a good thing Owen's okay, because I might have left his body down there with Samuel's. And the last thing I need to worry about is explaining murder by a paranormal."

Nick snickered.

"Anyway, the whole Owen debacle is why I came to Worthington Cove. I needed to sort things through and figure out what's next."

He studied her for a long moment. "Does *what's next* take you back to Oklahoma City?"

His gaze triggered an onslaught of heat that raced up to her neck and cheeks. Was he simply curious and making conversation? Or was he trying to gauge her intentions toward him—toward them?

"I have a life there. A career. And a house. But it doesn't feel like home anymore. It's just a place where I work and sleep."

"Well, I can tell you from firsthand experience that living in Worthington Cove has its virtues." A smile played on his lips. "The Chesapeake Bay, sailing, steamed crabs, Dempsy's, Aunt Margaret's cinnamon rolls." He hesitated. "Me."

"Oh, her rolls are absolutely the best, to be sure." Bethany grinned. "It'd be worth staying here just for breakfast at Horatio House. And…you're not so bad."

Nick laughed—a deep, infectious chortle. "Well, then, if I were you, I'd seriously consider it. For Aunt Margaret's rolls, if nothing else."

Then he moved his head closer to hers, so close his breath caressed her cheek. She latched onto every detail of his face: the bit of hair tumbling over his forehead, the stubble on his chin, and the curve of his lips. Her attention lingered on his lips, and she remembered their warmth and softness. She moistened her own, certain the moment would end in a kiss. But he stood and extended his hand to help her to her feet.

"We should go back to the inn before it gets completely dark."

"I know, but it's so peaceful here. I hate to leave."

He nodded, pulling her up. "It's the water. There's something calming about the way it continuously flows onward. Even when there's an obstruction, like a branch or a rock, the water always finds its way around it." He lightly squeezed her hand. "Because it's meant to be."

Like us? Her pulse raced once again, leaving her breathless and lightheaded. She stared at him, unable to speak, and he gathered her into his arms. This time, he captured her mouth with his. She closed her eyes and returned the kiss, her hands grasping his sides as she relished the smoothness of his lips and the slight roughness of his stubble. As they held each other, she smelled the familiar, comforting scent of sun and saltwater. His scent.

"We really should head back," he murmured between kisses. "Maybe we can talk more over a drink this evening."

"I'd like that."

"And dinner," he added, his lips still pressing against hers. "If you don't have plans."

"I don't have plans."

"Good." He kissed her once more, letting his mouth linger against hers before he pulled away. "Then I'll cook. You like steamed crabs?"

"I think so," Bethany said with uncertainty. "I like crabs, but I'm not sure I've ever had them steamed."

"Willing to take a chance?"

She smiled. "Are you a good cook?"

"Of course."

"Then you're on."

He grasped her hand and led her into the woods. "In that case, let's get going."

Chapter 17: Dinner at Nick's Place

Darkness had descended when Nick drove them along the narrow lane that wound through the woods surrounding his house. Although the headlights illuminated the white line marking the edge of the asphalt, large trees and wild undergrowth on both sides of the country road blocked any light from the night sky. Bethany glanced out the car window. The blackness masked any signs of civilization hidden behind the brush.

"This road sure is dark. Does anyone live out here besides you?"

"Believe it or not, quite a few people live out here," he replied. "But the county doesn't think it's enough people to justify putting in streetlights."

He slowed when they approached an old rural mailbox nailed to a massive wooden post, and turned onto a gravel driveway. Bethany glimpsed a light in the distance. As he drove farther in, a two-story cottage came into view just beyond the stand of trees.

He stopped the car and turned to her. "We're here. This is where I live."

She stared, surprised by the attractiveness of the quaint stone house. It was like something she'd see in a magazine. A porch and railing spanned the front, with an entryway illuminated by a pendant light hanging from a simple portico. Above it, a wide dormer jutted out from the center of the roof.

"Nick, this house…it's amazing."

Beaming, he took her hand as she got out of the car, and led her inside. "Let me show you around. The place is rather small, so it won't take long."

Bethany walked into the softly lit living room, furnished with an ocean-blue sofa and two off-white chairs facing a wall-mounted, big-screen TV. A large painting of a sailboat that looked a lot like the *Natalie Rose* hung on the wall behind the sofa.

"My great-great-grandfather, Harrison Dorsey, built this house in 1875. The family updated the original structure during the nineteen forties, adding electricity and running water. But that was the last time anyone did major work on the place until I started renovating it a year and a half ago."

She grinned. "You sound just like a museum tour guide."

"History is my thing, you know. I'm full of fun facts." He briefly scanned the room before turning his attention back to her. "The property borders on the Chesapeake Bay, and the cottage was used as a fishing lodge for the last twenty years. The place was a total wreck and needed a serious makeover when I inherited it."

"You've done a fantastic job. I love the coastal décor. It's cozy."

"Thank you. It's been a learning experience."

Nick ushered her into the kitchen. Above the antique kitchen sink, a large bow window framed the expanse of grass reaching down to the bay. At the water's edge, a lighted pier with a small sailboat tied alongside it led to a large deck surrounded by water.

"The window is new, along with pier and deck."

"What a gorgeous view." She waved her hand toward the window. "Is that the *Pipsqueak*?"

He chuckled. "Sure is. That little boat holds a special place in my heart, and I don't think I'll ever be able to let her go. I felt the same way about a lot of the cottage's vintage fixtures and furniture, too."

"Like the sink?"

"Yep, and that big cupboard next to it, which dates back to the nineteen thirties. It's called a Hoosier cabinet. The predecessor of built-in kitchen cabinets." He shot Bethany his lopsided grin and pointed to the sleek electric range and stainless-steel refrigerator against the wall. "But I'm not opposed to conveniences like modern appliances and indoor plumbing." He motioned to a narrow stairway off the kitchen. "And, by the way, the bathroom is upstairs."

"With a claw-foot tub, I suppose?"

"Of course, but a new one," he said, smiling. "The original was unsalvageable. The bedrooms are upstairs, too. I sleep in one and use the spare as my office."

She turned back to the kitchen window and a pang of envy struck her as she studied the view. His home was perfect. A paradise. So unlike her little house, which sat on a tiny plot of grass on a street with dozens of similar homes lined up in a row.

"The cottage is very charming. You're very lucky to have a house with the bay right outside your back door. It suits you."

"I can't picture living anywhere else." He opened the refrigerator and retrieved two bottles of pale ale. "Beer's a must, since we're having steamed crabs." He handed a bottle to Bethany. "I set a couple of traps off the pier yesterday morning. Let's go check them."

They walked out to the pier deck. She grabbed a spot at the wooden picnic table and watched as Nick pulled two wire cages out of the water.

"We got some good ones," he said, measuring and tossing one crab after another into a bushel basket. "Plenty for the two of us."

After setting up the steamer pot on a propane camping stove and adding the crabs, Nick sat across the table from her, his body illuminated by the soft glow of the miniature lanterns on the deck railing. While waiting for the crabs to cook, they talked about his job with the conservation group and her work at the institute. In the distance, red and white beacons atop the Chesapeake Bay Bridge's suspension towers cast reflections in the dark expanse of water.

As Nick moved on to stories about growing up in Worthington Cove, Bethany sipped her beer and breathed in the scent of crab seasoning. She could sit here every evening, soaking up the magic of the Chesapeake, Worthington Cove, and Nick. This version of him was endearing. He was relaxed and content, as though this place—the house, the water, the town— grounded him. And he responded to it with the care and respect one would show a valued family member.

Barely any time passed before Nick stood, checked the pot, then dumped the crabs onto the brown kraft paper lining the table. Bethany looked at the pile, taken aback by the red, spider-like bodies covered with seasoning, and frowned. How were they supposed to *eat* these?

A grin played on Nick's lips. "Are you going to try one? I can pick it for you."

She gingerly touched the nearest one. "This one looks good. Honestly, they all look the same to me."

His eyes reflected amusement. "I meant I'll pick the meat out of the shell for you. Picking crabs is an art, you know. It requires skill and finesse. But I have no doubts you'll get the hang of it, because I'm an excellent teacher."

"What a coincidence. That's exactly what I need, a crab-picking lesson from someone knowledgeable. Because I have absolutely no idea where to start."

"It's easy once you know the trick." Chuckling, he slid next to her, grabbed a crab, and somehow opened the bright red shell. Then, with deft fingers, he extracted bits of white meat and set them on her plate. After picking a sizable mound of meat for her, he reached into the cooler and grabbed two more beers, then started on a crab for himself.

"I keep thinking about what happened to Owen today," Nick said after they'd devoured the last crab. "I've never witnessed a haunting like that, when a spirit moves a heavy object."

"I suppose the energy from Samuel's anger was strong enough to pull Owen up the steps."

"He must have been terrified."

Bethany laughed. "Yeah, I'm sure he was."

She ran her fingers over the tiny bruises Owen had left on her forearm, relieved he'd accepted their relationship was over, but still angry over his behavior. The aggressiveness had shocked her. He'd never physically hurt her before, and she never imagined he was capable of such roughness. But then, she hadn't expected him to be a liar and a cheat. What a package he turned out to be. Thank god he was gone for good.

"He deserved it, though," she mused. "And I will be forever grateful to Samuel for literally dragging him out of my life."

"Me too." He flashed her his endearing, lopsided grin and gulped his beer. "Think you'll go back to the root cellar?"

"I can't give up now. Today's search was anything but productive. I barely made any progress, and there's still a lot left to sift through. Besides," she added, "I'm pretty sure Samuel will keep the jerks and idiots out of my way."

"I wouldn't want to cross him, that's for sure." Nick chuckled, then downed the last of his beer. He picked up the empty bottles and tossed them into a nearby bucket, pulled two more out of the cooler, and offered one to Bethany. "It's such a pleasant night. Want to hang out here a while longer?"

"Sounds nice," she said, holding up the bottle. "Here's to Samuel."

"I'll drink to that." Nick clinked her bottle and took a swig. "How about tomorrow? You want some help in the root cellar? I'm pretty good with a hand rake and trowel."

"Hmm." She arched a brow. "How good are you at calming wayward spirits?"

"Very good. Haven't had one yank me out of a room." He smirked and his eyes danced. "Not yet, anyway."

"Then you're hired."

"I'll be drawing water samples from Carter Creek in the morning, but I'll have some free time in the afternoon." He raised his brows questioningly. "Meet me at Horatio House around one?"

She nodded, elated to be spending more time with him. "I can't wait to get back down there and finish the search. The sooner we can provide Samuel with closure, the better."

"When we prove he was murdered, think Samuel will…you know…cross over?" Nick asked.

She snickered. "Like walking into the light?"

He gave her arm a playful push. "I know nothing about the spirit world and how it works."

"Really? I'd have thought you would know all about it."

"You're the one who talks to ghosts, not me."

"I have no idea what will happen. But my guess is that he'll do what's best for him, which could mean staying here to watch over his home like he's been doing for the past two hundred and fifty years."

"Aunt Margaret wouldn't mind. She'd miss him if he left. Signs of his presence at Horatio House give her something to talk about. And they draw attention to the inn and bring in guests. Apparently, quite a few people like to stay at haunted hotels."

"I'd miss him, too, now that I'm getting to know him." Bethany picked at the label on her beer, surprised at the tenderness Samuel stirred within her. "There's a connection between us, like something I'd have with an older brother or a favorite uncle. He's family."

"You know, once we reveal the truth about his death, he won't have a reason to stay." Nick grasped her hand and focused on her face, his deep brown eyes searching hers. "What about you? After we find his ring, is there a reason for you to stay?"

His question stabbed at her chest. There were many reasons to stay, and most of them pointed back to Nick.

He felt familiar, like home, and her stomach twisted at the thought of leaving him. But a portion of her brain still expected him to ghost her again. Before seriously considering a life here with him, she needed to know what happened after that summer.

A small smile touched her lips as she replied. "I hope so."

****

After clearing the remnants of dinner, Nick grabbed a blanket and a flashlight, and they walked up the narrow stretch of beach that extended along his property. Just before the point where the sand ended and vegetation overtook the shoreline, he spread the blanket and they sat shoulder to shoulder, watching the waves. Hundreds of stars in the night sky silently stood guard over the swells that gently encroached upon the sand, then receded. The hypnotic rhythm of the surf filled Bethany with an overwhelming sense of tranquility.

Nick reached for her hand, entwining his fingers in hers. "I keep thinking about that summer."

Her heart skipped. "The last time I was here? Ten years ago?"

"Yeah, that one."

She stiffened. *Is this it? Is he finally going to tell me what happened?* "I think about it too."

"Do you remember the night we went to Ridgely Park after dinner at Verrazano's? When we first kissed?" He stared out at the inky black water as he spoke, his profile illuminated by the deck lanterns farther down the beach.

She laid her head against his shoulder. "I do. You were my first crush."

"I've never forgotten those kisses. As chaste as they

were, they took my breath away." He snaked his arm around her waist and pulled her closer. "You still take my breath away."

Her body shivered at his touch, and a rush of emotions soared through her veins: affection, joy, desire, doubt, and fear. She could picture a future with Nick. They'd been friends, they still were, and the possibility of them being so much more felt within reach. All she needed was an explanation. To know why he had ghosted her.

Bethany glanced away and studied the tendrils of foamy seawater rushing toward their toes.

"It'd be so easy to fall for you again," she whispered. "But my crush on you left me shattered. And I can't handle another heartbreak right now."

He grasped her hand and stared out at the bay, absently stroking her thumb with his as though contemplating her words.

"What we shared that summer was amazing. I loved you with all my heart and never meant to hurt you. I wish I'd handled things better."

She squeezed her eyes shut and forced herself to speak. "What happened, Nick? You were supposed to call me. We were going to text. But all I got was silence." Her heart pounded as she studied the surf receding into the bay and braced herself for whatever he might say.

"Right after you left, Natalie got sick." He paused, swiping a sprig of dark hair away from his forehead. "She'd been battling leukemia for several years and had a relapse. We thought she was going to be okay, but several weeks later, she passed away."

Bethany gasped. *Oh, my god! Natalie died?* "Nick, I'm so sorry."

Without thinking, she wrapped her arms around him, holding on tightly as if the embrace could ease all the pain caused by his loss. He relaxed against her, his breath faint against her neck. Neither said a word. They just held on to each other. Time seemed to stop as the moment stretched on. And then Nick's voice broke the stillness.

"Her death devastated all of us. We thought she'd pull through again. And then…she was gone." He broke away, holding Bethany's gaze while closing his fingers around hers. "I wanted to call you. Hear your voice. Feel your presence. But my world had become a dark place. I was a wreck. Furious with the doctors, the hospital staff, everyone and everything. I wanted to let go of my anger, shake off the darkness and get a handle on my emotional state before I talked to you. It took longer than I expected. December came and went, then April and May. When summer started, I knew you'd be back, like always. I had my apology all planned. As soon as I saw you, I'd explain what happened. You'd forgive me, and then we'd sail to Matapeake Beach in the *Pipsqueak* and have a romantic picnic lunch. Start again where we left off. I even bought you a promise ring. But then—"

"I never showed up." An ache formed in her chest, a deep, hollowed-out void that quickly filled with guilt and remorse. He hadn't abandoned her. Didn't discard her for someone prettier or smarter. He'd lost his sister.

"I thought you'd dumped me." She swiped at her eyes. "I couldn't bear the possibility of running into you. It would've hurt too much. So I stayed away."

Nick gently pulled her against his chest and brushed his lips against her forehead. "All this time, I've regretted my stupid teenage decisions. I wanted things between us to work. More than anything. But I was a kid trying to navigate a romance with over a thousand miles between us, and completely unprepared for what happened."

His words unleashed an onslaught of tears. If only he had left a message, said something. She would have understood. Been the supportive girlfriend he had needed. But she'd been so wrapped up in her own grief that she never thought something might be wrong in his life. Never considered reaching out and giving him a chance to explain. And it had cost them each a broken heart.

Gently, he lifted her chin and wiped her cheek with his finger. "Bethany, seeing you again made me realize my feelings for you haven't changed. You captured my heart the first time I saw you in Dempsy's, when your flip-flop landed at my feet. And my heart still belongs to you."

Regret clutched her throat. If she'd known, she would have come back to Worthington Cove. Their teenage crush could have developed into so much more—a life that included Nick.

"Nick, I—"

"Bethany," he interrupted, his eyes intense. "I know you've only been here for a week, but our connection is still as strong as it was when we were kids." He exhaled and stroked her bottom lip with his thumb. "Being with you feels right, and I'm not ready to let you go."

"Nick, I—"

"I need more time with you. As much as you'll give me."

"Nick, I—"

"So I'm just going to ask. Will you give our romance

another chance?"

She looped her arms around his neck and placed her finger against his lips.

"Nick, I don't want to let you go, either. Things are better when I'm with you." She brushed her lips against his cheek, savoring his briny, sun-kissed scent. "After all, you're just too darned cute. And a great kisser. Plus, you have a sailboat. What more could a girl want?"

"This time, I promise to let you know if something terrible happens that turns my life upside down."

"You better, Nick Dorsey."

He shifted, sighing deeply as he captured her lips with his. She tasted crab seasoning and beer as she leaned into the kiss. Gently, he lowered her until they were facing each other on the blanket. With eyes closed, face hot, and breath erratic, she slid her hand down his spine and pulled him closer, leaving no space between his body and hers. His heart pounded against her chest, his pulse in sync with hers, and she deepened the kiss, savoring his touch, taste, and texture.

The warmth of his mouth and hands ignited an uncontrolled burn that sent a stream of fire throughout her body. Long-dormant nerve endings popped and sizzled. The conflagration left her lightheaded, insatiable, and aching for more. She paused, gasping for air, then heard his voice, breathless and pressing, floating between them.

"You mentioned Oklahoma City didn't feel like home anymore. Can you see yourself here? In Worthington Cove? With me?"

He pulled away and studied her, his charcoal eyes surveying hers as he brushed his fingers along the edge of her chin.

The question, barely audible over the sounds of the bay, hung over her, its weight constricting her breath. She didn't answer immediately. Instead, she listened to the surf, letting the soft whoosh of the gentle breakers temper her pulse and clear her head.

Could she visualize herself here? *Yes.*

Was a relationship with Nick a reason to uproot her life? *Yes.*

Aside from her tiny house and her job at the institute, there was nothing keeping her in Oklahoma. Her world there had revolved around Owen and *his* friends, *his* activities, *his* career. But that life was over. It was time to live for herself without letting fear—of change *or* heartbreak—hold her back.

Bethany caught his hand and pressed his fingers against her cheek. "I can picture a life here with you. But following through would be a big step. One that's exciting and perfect, but also scary and overwhelming. It's a lot to process."

He pressed his lips against her forehead. "I bet it is. But if you decide it's something you want to do, I'm here to give you all the support you need."

Then he drew her even closer, his eyes smoldering as he reclaimed her mouth with his. As she lost herself in his kiss, the apprehension squeezing her chest began to dissipate.

****

The grandfather clock in the library delivered two deep-pitched bongs as Bethany slipped into her bed at Horatio House. Once under the quilts, she stroked her lips, recalling the pressure of Nick's mouth and body against hers. His touch, urgent and electrifying, had left her euphoric and wanting more. But it was the depth of his affection that gave her the courage to consider staying in Worthington Cove and building a life here with him. Still thinking of Nick, and the way his eyes had burned with desire for her, Bethany drifted to sleep.

"What a wretched excuse for a man." Samuel's voice resonated with disdain.

Bethany's eyes flew open, and she bolted upright. In the dimness, she spied him pacing the floor at the foot of her bed.

"What?" she asked, disoriented by the abrupt awakening. "How can you say that about Nick?"

"No, not Mr. Dorsey. You misunderstand." Samuel's mouth puckered into a glower as he perched on the edge of her mattress. "I'm referring to the sniveling degenerate who bullied you in the root cellar this afternoon." He snorted. "Your former betrothed."

"Oh. You mean Owen." She leaned back against the pillows. "Thankfully, he left late this afternoon. After his encounter with you."

"Ah, yes." Samuel's scowl softened, and a smug grin touched his lips. "Assisting with his departure was quite satisfying, although I must apologize again for getting carried away. The man had no civility. And frankly, Miss Bethany, I don't understand why you favored him."

"I've been asking myself the same thing."

Pulling the quilts closer to her chin, Bethany attempted to describe her relationship with Owen. "When I first met him, I thought he was a good person, and I respected him. But he didn't turn out to be the man I thought he was."

"He certainly wasn't worthy of your esteem." Samuel studied her. "You deserve to be highly regarded by your suitors. And nothing less."

She smiled at his declaration. "I think Owen did value me. At first. But as his career flourished and he grew more and more successful, he viewed himself as extremely important. Much more important than me, apparently."

"Ah. He allowed his ego to become his master. I've seen many men succumb to an exaggerated perception of their greatness."

"Yep. That sounds about right." Her thoughts turned to Owen's comments in the root cellar. Until that moment, she hadn't recognized how different he'd become. That he'd started viewing her as his property. The shift had occurred over time, and the magnitude of his transformation was disturbing. "The thing is, I hadn't realized how much he'd changed. Sometimes love blinds us to the truth."

He nodded, avoiding her gaze and instead directing his attention to the wall. "That comment, I suppose, applies to me as well. Luckily, you perceived his true nature before your life crumbled under the weight of deception. I, however, was not so fortunate." His hazel eyes glistened with unshed tears.

Without thinking, Bethany cast the quilts aside and threw her arms around him. His skin was icy, and she shivered as a chill coursed through her. But she didn't release him. Instead, she tightened her embrace and held on, loathing Frederick Howard for taking his life. Tears cascaded down her cheeks and wet the rough cotton fabric of his shirt.

"Ariella loved you, Samuel. I'm absolutely sure of it. And if she hid the truth about your son, it was to protect you. I know in my heart that she never meant to hurt you. The villain was Frederick Howard. He acted alone when he murdered you. And Ariella, unfortunately, was caught in the fallout." Bethany pulled back, scrutinizing him. "For your own sake, you have to believe that."

He choked down a sob. "I will make an attempt."

"In the meantime, Nick and I will keep searching for your ring in the root cellar. And we will locate your remains." She grasped his frigid hand. "What will happen to you when we reveal the truth about your death?"

He stood and resumed pacing. "That knowledge eludes me, I'm afraid, since I'm not well versed in the principles that govern my existence. I'd like to stay here. This is my home, after all. But I may have no choice but to continue into the next phase of my afterlife."

A sad smile touched her lips. "Mrs. Snowden will miss you terribly if you move on. So will I."

He paused mid-step and studied her. "After you recover my remains, will you ensure they're laid to rest in the family cemetery?"

"Of course."

Sorrow weighed down his features as he dipped his chin, acknowledging her reply. "And what will you do, Miss Bethany? Do you plan to leave Horatio House and go back to…?"

"Oklahoma? Aunt Ginny asked me to stay in Worthington Cove and live with her. I love this town, and my family's history is here. But I don't know if I have the courage to leave the life I have there."

"But there's Mr. Dorsey to consider." Samuel's face brightened. "He seems quite smitten with you, and I certainly approve of a connection with him. The man is quite admirable. He's been very supportive of your endeavor to find me."

A blush heated Bethany's cheeks as she recalled the kisses she'd shared with Nick. "I like him, too. Quite a bit, actually."

"Then your choice should be easy. Remain in Worthington Cove. It appears everyone you care about is here."

She considered his words. Stay here with the people she cared about. Could her decision really be that simple?

"But I have a house in Oklahoma City. A career."

Samuel stopped pacing. "I'm certain that houses and employment are available in Worthington Cove. Unless..." He leaned in and scanned her face. "Are you truly happy there? More so than you would be if you lived here?"

Would she be happy there? Owen had been the center of her universe. And that world had collapsed when she finally saw him for who he was. Nothing about that life was worth preserving. She'd be starting over no matter where she chose to be.

So why was she hesitant about taking a chance and beginning a new life here that included Nick?

"Honestly, I'd probably be miserable back in Oklahoma."

"Well then, trust your heart, Miss Bethany. Because to me, it appears returning to a place that holds nothing but misery would be an unsuitable course of action."

Chapter 18: What Really Happened to Samuel Watts

The loud knock woke her. Then she heard Mrs. Snowden's voice from the other side of the bedroom door.

"Bethany, dear, are you awake?"

Fuzzy with sleep, Bethany swung her legs from under the covers and stumbled to the door. Mrs. Snowden greeted her with a tentative smile.

"I'm sorry if I woke you, dear. But Nick's in the kitchen and he's mumbling something about finding Samuel's ring in the root cellar."

"Why is he here so early?" Bethany yawned and rubbed her eyes. "We were going down there after lunch."

The innkeeper scrutinized her. "It's one o'clock in the afternoon, dear."

"What?" She shook her head, barely comprehending Mrs. Snowden's words. "I've slept through the entire morning?" *Dammit!* She'd wanted to reach out to Aunt Ginny this morning about the town council meeting tonight.

"That's okay, dear." Mrs. Snowden pulled Bethany into a motherly embrace. "Yesterday must have been exhausting. Judging from Owen's foul mood when he came back, the outing in the root cellar didn't go very well at all. I've never seen anyone pack and leave so quickly. His behavior was quite alarming, actually." She stepped back and frowned. "What happened down there? I'm dying to know."

"It's a long story," Bethany replied, smiling. "But he got a taste of Samuel's temper."

"Oh?" Mrs. Snowden raised her brows. "This I need to hear."

Bethany looked down at her hands, unsure of where to start. Although she had witnessed the incident in the root cellar, she still had a hard time believing what she had seen. It went far beyond the cold drafts and lingering wafts of lavender she'd encountered in the house.

"The first time I went down into the root cellar, I sensed Samuel was there. There were signs—like sudden pockets of cold air, the smell of lavender and pipe tobacco, and whispers. Initially, I was skeptical. I didn't believe in ghosts and figured I was imagining things. But Samuel's presence grew stronger. Both in the house and in the root cellar."

Mrs. Snowden nodded. "Lately, I've felt him more than I normally do."

"Eventually, all the signs convinced me his spirit is real. And yesterday, in the root cellar, Owen experienced the full strength of Samuel's manifestation." Bethany inhaled and looked directly at Mrs. Snowden. "Owen made Samuel angry. Livid, in fact. And Samuel's response was physical."

The color drained from the innkeeper's face. "Oh, my! Samuel's never bothered my guests before. Ever. What on earth did Owen do to provoke him?"

"His behavior toward me turned somewhat aggressive, and Samuel reacted…protectively." Bethany recounted everything that happened, including Owen's forcible attempt to bring her back to the inn and the details of his expulsion from the root cellar.

Mrs. Snowden studied her. "Are you okay?"

"Yeah. I didn't want to run into Owen at the inn after everything that happened, so I took a walk through the woods to find the stream. And I got lost. Somehow, Nick tracked me down."

"I'm grateful he found you so quickly. He knows this property like the back of his hand. But..." She frowned. "I also blame him for taking you back to the root cellar after that first day. I never thought it was a good idea."

"It's my fault. I was being stubborn. Nick was only looking out for me because I insisted on going back."

"Maybe I should hold you both accountable," Mrs. Snowden said with a sigh. "And, for the record, I'm not thrilled that you two are planning to go back again to look for Samuel's ring."

"I promise we'll be fine."

"I suppose so, if you stay in Samuel's good graces." She flashed Bethany a warm smile. "I must admit, I've thoroughly enjoyed all the excitement. And I know Nick has, too. He rarely spends time here, because work keeps him busy. Usually, he'll stop in once a week to scan the guest list and check to see if any of the rooms I've booked need maintenance. But when he found out you were coming, he showed up the day you were due to check in and has been back every day since. And I'm glad. Having him around and seeing him so happy just warms my heart."

Bethany's chest buzzed with joy. Nick had known she was coming and made a point to be here. To see her.

"Anyway, I'd better let you get dressed." Mrs. Snowden turned toward the stairs. "I'll tell Nick you'll be down shortly."

Twenty minutes later, Bethany bounded down the stairs, eager to see Nick and resume the search for Samuel.

"It's about time you showed up, sleepyhead." He chuckled, and her heart pounded at the memory of last night's kisses—the softness of his lips and the caress of his hands exploring her skin.

"Sorry." She poured coffee and slid into the chair across from him, struggling to slow her racing pulse. "I had no idea how late it was."

"Bethany, dear." Mrs. Snowden's voice. "I meant to ask you earlier, but it slipped my mind. What are your plans for tomorrow?"

Tomorrow? Bethany swallowed a mouthful of coffee and glanced at Nick. "If we don't find the ring today, I guess we'll go back to the root cellar tomorrow."

"I was referring to your stay here. You're due to check out in the morning, but your room is available if you want to stay longer."

Bethany froze, her coffee mug suspended in midair as she stared at Mrs. Snowden. Had it been a week already?

"You're leaving tomorrow." Nick's voice was flat, making an observation rather than asking a question. She glanced over and found him watching her, his body still and his expression indecipherable.

"I'd bought a round-trip ticket. The return flight leaves tomorrow evening, around seven."

The thought of getting on a plane back to Oklahoma City sent a jolt to her gut. She wasn't ready to leave Worthington Cove. Not yet. She needed more time to explore her relationship with Nick and figure out what happens next.

And they had to find Samuel's ring.

The room's temperature dipped, and a delicate draft followed, ruffling the stack of napkins on the table as it wafted through the kitchen. Then Samuel's voice touched her thoughts.

"Can it be true? Today is your last day here? Then you must find my ring immediately. It's of the utmost importance."

Bethany took another gulp of coffee and stood. "Mrs. Snowden, I'll let you know later today about extending my stay."

Then she turned toward Nick. "We'd better get moving. We have a lot to sift through and not much time."

****

As they hiked to the root cellar, a flutter of shadows from the bright sun animated the thicket. But the beauty of the autumn afternoon was lost on Bethany. Instead, the trip back to Oklahoma City consumed her thoughts. Tomorrow was too soon to leave. She could reschedule her flight for the weekend. Extend her time off from the office. She had plenty of vacation days left.

But what if they didn't find the ring? She couldn't keep postponing her return and asking Mrs. Snowden for additional nights. At some point she had to decide: either stay and move forward with a new life here, or go back and continue living the old one. But the thought of putting one or the other into motion left her petrified. What if she made the wrong choice?

Samuel had told her to trust her heart. Why was that so difficult?

Nick stopped when they reached the cellar entrance.

Instead of opening the old wooden door, he grasped Bethany's hands. Startled at the gesture, she glanced up and found him peering down at her with an intensity that was serious, yet vulnerable. He searched her face, his brown eyes earnest, and she stared back, unable to look away.

"I hate that your flight home is tomorrow." He wrapped his arms around her waist. "I'm afraid of losing you again."

She snuggled in, laying her cheek against his chest and listening to the sound of his heartbeat. The warmth of his embrace felt comfortable. Familiar and perfect. Like the universe had designed him specifically for her. She'd felt the same way ten years ago, when they'd held each other on her last night here. She'd hated leaving him then and didn't want to do it tomorrow.

He smoothed her hair with his palm, then kissed her forehead, letting his lips linger there for several seconds before pulling away to open the cellar door and start down the stone steps. When he reached the dirt floor, he fished fresh batteries out of his backpack and inserted them into the lantern and two flashlights that lay on the floor.

Bethany walked up behind him. "About tomorrow."

He turned, his eyes filled with hope.

"I don't want to go back yet. But—"

Nick pulled her toward him and pressed his nose against hers. "Let's forget about the *buts* for now and think about *what could be* instead."

His mouth immediately found hers, and her protest faded at the touch. She breathed in as she returned this kiss, inhaling the salty, sun-kissed scent of his skin mixed with a trace of something else. Familiar, but not

Nick's scent. Lavender and pipe tobacco?

Before her mind could fully process the implication of lavender, the air turned colder. She drew back instinctively and saw wisps of fog escaping her lips. *No. Not now!*

"What's wrong?" Nick frowned as she stepped away from him.

Icy fingers rested on her shoulders, and her entire body shivered in response. Then a disapproving voice pushed into her head.

"*Miss Bethany, this is hardly an appropriate circumstance for lovemaking. You must focus on locating my ring. We haven't much time.*"

"Samuel's here, reminding me it's time for us to get to work."

"Ah. He's such a killjoy," Nick muttered as he leaned in to kiss her once more. "But he has a point."

She was grinning when Nick backed away, but her lighthearted mood faltered as she surveyed the floor. A large section of the marked plot on the right side of the root cellar remained untouched. "I didn't get much done while you were gone. Owen threw me off track."

"He threw us both off track." Nick snorted. "But on the positive side, it gave Samuel the opportunity to get rid of him."

"He did, all right. And I'm very grateful for that." Bethany pulled on her garden gloves and scowled. "But we have a lot more dirt to sift through. More than half of the second plot we outlined."

"Then the ring has to be in that section." Nick pointed to the undisturbed soil. "Let's start where you left off."

He moved the lantern closer to their work area while

she grabbed the hand rake and kneeled beside the untouched patch of soil. Raking and sifting in the quiet with Nick felt comfortable—as though they'd always been together—and the thought of resuming her life without him twisted her stomach into knots. So why was she hesitant to commit to a life in Worthington Cove?

Nick was right. She needed to focus on what *could be*, such as forging a long-term relationship with a man who was kind and supportive—a best friend and partner who would be there for her no matter what. More than anything, she wanted someone who loved her for herself rather than her career and community standing. And she wanted to live surrounded by family and friends.

She could be happy. Here. With Nick.

Only when her shoulders ached and her fingers were stiff from slashing at the earthen floor did Bethany straighten and assess their progress. Although they'd sifted through a good portion of the marked space, their efforts had uncovered nothing more than a few shards of hardened clay, and a sizable swath of untouched floor still loomed in front of them. She stretched her fingers to loosen the kinks and turned toward Nick.

"There's so much more to do. It'll take several more hours to sift through what's left, and my hands are telling me they're done."

He grasped her hand and gently kneaded her fingers. "How about I keep going while you rest?"

Bethany glanced at her watch. "I can't, Nick. It's getting late, and Aunt Ginny is expecting me to attend the town council meeting tonight."

"Ready to call it a day, then?"

"I think so."

As she stood, the air grew frosty, and Bethany

sensed a frigid pressure on her shoulder blades.

"*Don't stop now, Miss Bethany.*" Samuel's voice crept into her head. "*You're so close.*"

Nick looked up, frowning, his breath visible in the lantern light. "It's getting cold again. Samuel's back, isn't he?"

"He knows I'm ready to stop."

An icy draft skimmed the back of her neck.

"*Miss Bethany, don't leave me down here. I couldn't bear it.*"

Samuel's words stabbed at her heart. She'd vowed to find him, and he trusted her to see it through. Abandoning him wasn't an option. But she'd also agreed to discuss the history festival program with the planning committee, and she couldn't disappoint Aunt Ginny. The only way to honor both commitments was to attend the meeting tonight and come back to the root cellar early tomorrow.

That's what she'd do. Return in the morning, even if it meant postponing her flight.

"I hate to leave, but Aunt Ginny's counting on me to give the council members feedback on their plans for the history festival. I have to go. But—"

"*No! You promised me! You must continue the search!*"

Samuel's words, determined and passionate, resonated inside her skull as a blast of biting air slapped her face. Bethany shivered, uneasy with the panic in his voice as the air picked up speed and the temperature dropped even lower.

Nick stood and pulled her against him, frowning. "What's going on? It feels like a winter storm's coming."

"Samuel's upset. He wants me to stay down here

and continue searching for his ring. I wish I could, but I'm—"

She tried to tell him her plan. But the rotating force grew stronger, and the momentum of the swirling air swallowed her words. Soon, sparks of static electricity crackled and snapped at her skin and the smell of ozone—the precursor to a thunderstorm—filled the space. She clung to Nick, her heart thudding with fear as icy gusts swept past her cheeks.

"You can't go, Miss Bethany. I need you!"

She gasped at the sound of Samuel's voice, strong and vibrating with desperation. It sounded even more powerful than when he'd spoken aloud to Owen.

Nick looked at her, stunned. "Is… is that Samuel?"

Bethany nodded as the gale circulated faster and faster, picking up bits of clay and sand with each pass. A storm was brewing, and they were stranded in the middle of it. Dirt clogged the air, leaving nothing visible except for a dull, eerie glow from the flashlights. She covered her face with her hands, gasping for breath as Nick held her against his chest to shield her from the onslaught. Dread gripped her as detritus from the cellar floor crashed into them.

"I've never seen him this worked up before," Bethany said, her voice shaking. "Should we leave?"

"It's too hard to find our way out right now. Let's stay put for another minute. He may calm down by then."

"I hope so. This is terrifying."

"Yeah." Nick tightened his hold on her. "But don't worry. We'll be okay."

And then something large—the trowel?—flew past her head and slammed into Nick. She felt him flinch and glanced up to see a gaping gash on the right side of his forehead. Anger surged through her at the sight of blood running down the side of his cheek.

Samuel had gone too far.

Bethany turned and shouted into the dust cloud. "Samuel. Enough! You better stop this *now*. Nick's hurt! He's bleeding."

A quiet sob floated into her thoughts, followed by words spoken with remorse.

"Oh, dear lord! What have I done?"

The tempest quieted as suddenly as it had appeared, leaving the air calm and still. She wiped the dirt from her face as the dust settled around them and examined Nick's head wound, relieved that the bleeding was subsiding and the cut wasn't too deep.

"Nick, are you all right?"

"Yeah, I think so." He swiped at his blood- and dirt-encrusted forehead before grabbing the overturned lantern and surveying the cellar. Samuel's outburst had swept away swaths of soil, leaving the floor raw and uneven, with irregular mounds of pebbles and sand piled against the walls. Nick leaned down to scrutinize something in one of the newly formed gouges in front of him and drew in a breath.

"Bethany, I see something." He picked up a flashlight and, kneeling, trained its beam on a small bump protruding from the soil. "See that chunk of dirt? There's something odd about it. Like it's covering something."

He set the lantern next to it and rubbed at the bulge with his index finger. As the dirt fell away, a sliver of dull gold appeared. With slow, cautious strokes, Nick brushed off more dirt and exposed the surface of a miniature gold coin.

"Bethany, this could be it!" He carefully dislodged more soil until the shoulders of a gold shank became visible. After a few more swipes, he stopped and withdrew his hand, his face noticeably pale, even in the dim light.

Bethany kneeled next to him and stared down at the floor. Dirt still concealed a portion of the emblem engraved on the coin, but Bethany could make out a "W" on its bezel. Underneath the coin, a slender finger bone rested inside a circular gold band.

Neither uttered a word as they stared at the partially exposed ring. Minutes passed before Bethany finally found her voice. And then all she could manage was a whisper. "It's the one Samuel's wearing in the portrait."

The ring proved his story was true. Samuel wasn't lost at sea. He was murdered and buried in the root cellar.

A dull ache throbbed within her. She'd developed a strong attachment to the passionate man who appeared very much alive in her dreams. But the skeletal finger was a stark reminder that Samuel had died long ago. She swallowed a sob.

The air grew cold again, and she expected to hear Samuel's voice once more. But the chill was fleeting, and Nick's steady breath was the only sound she heard.

He laid his hand on her shoulder, and she looked up to find him studying her.

"Are you all right?"

Bethany wiped the tears running down her cheeks. "He seemed so alive. It's just hard to accept that he's actually a two-hundred-year-old skeleton buried here."

Nick pulled her closer and rested his forehead against hers. "His spirit *was* here, even though he wasn't living flesh and blood. We both sensed him. Especially you." He paused and strengthened his embrace. "But now that we've unearthed his remains and revealed the truth about his death, he could have moved on. We might not encounter him again."

"I know."

"And if that's the case, you're the one who helped him resolve the issues that kept him here. That's an amazing experience most people never have."

She continued to gaze at the ring, resisting the urge to run her finger over the engraved initial. Nick was right. Samuel's presence had been a gift. She had grown fond of him and hoped he'd found peace before moving to the next stop in his afterlife, whatever that might be.

"What should we do next?" she asked.

"I'm reluctant to disturb any more of his remains. For now, we should pack up our stuff and go back to the house." Nick stood, holding out his hand to help her to her feet. "Once we're there, I'll call the sheriff's office. Tell them what we discovered and ask them how to proceed."

Chapter 19: Is Horatio House Still Haunted?

The Horatio House kitchen, scented with hints of cinnamon and freshly brewed coffee, was still warm from the oven's last batch of pastry. However, the mood was somber as Bethany, Nick, and Mrs. Snowden huddled around the dinette table.

"The sheriff's department is sending an officer out tomorrow," Nick said. "I should probably contact the county's historical society, too. They may want an archaeologist to survey the site."

"Samuel wants to be buried in the family cemetery," Bethany added. "I think we need to honor his wishes."

A wisp of cold air brushed against Bethany's cheek, and she straightened. Could Samuel still be here? She glanced at Mrs. Snowden, but the innkeeper showed no signs of experiencing an icy draft. Instead, she reached over and patted Bethany's hand.

"Don't worry, dear. I'm sure we can do that for him once the authorities are done with their work." Mrs. Snowden hesitated, her eyes still on Bethany. "Have you decided what you're going to do next?"

Bethany felt Nick's gaze from across the table, and her throat tightened. Now that they'd found Samuel's ring, there wasn't a pressing reason to prolong her stay. She'd attend the town council meeting tonight and fulfill her obligation to Aunt Ginny. Then catch her flight back to Oklahoma City tomorrow evening. Return to her empty house. Go back to the institute and resume the same job she'd done for the past several years.

The thought of leaving filled her chest with a heavy weight.

"Aunt Ginny asked for my input on the town's plans for the history festival, and wants me to share my thoughts tonight at the town council meeting. She said they may hire someone to organize it." Bethany glanced at Nick. "If so, she wants me to apply for the job."

His face broke into the familiar lopsided grin. "I think you should."

"I agree, Miss Bethany."

Samuel? The words were fleeting, leaving Bethany to question whether she'd actually heard them.

"I'm also attending tonight's meeting," Mrs. Snowden said. "It's at the town library. We can walk over together."

"Mind if I tag along?" Nick asked.

"That'd be great." The innkeeper chuckled. "But be warned. The history festival planning committee will be there. They'll interpret your presence as an offer to volunteer for the festival and will have no qualms about assigning you an extensive to-do list."

Nick glanced across the table at Bethany, his brown eyes gleaming as he winked at her. "Warning acknowledged."

With a laugh, Mrs. Snowden went to the refrigerator and pulled out an assortment of lunch meats and cheeses, as well as mayonnaise, mustard, lettuce, and sliced tomatoes, and set them on the counter. Then she retrieved a loaf of bread and a large bag of potato chips from a drawer.

"Tonight, dinner is on me." She grabbed three plates

from a nearby cabinet and motioned toward the counter. "But it's self-serve. I hope you don't mind sandwiches. You can heat them in the toaster oven."

****

When Bethany, Nick, and Mrs. Snowden entered the library's meeting room, most of the council and planning committee members had taken their places at the large wooden table. Bethany slid into the chair next to Aunt Ginny while Nick claimed the one beside her. He grasped her hand and interlaced his fingers with hers. She welcomed his touch, finding comfort in the warmth of his skin and the strength of his grip. He was there for *her* and his support was unconditional. How could she leave him and return to Oklahoma City?

Aunt Ginny introduced her to the group, then gave everyone a copy of Bethany's notes on the original plan. As they read through the packets, Bethany scanned the attendees' faces, trying to gauge their reactions. Would they consider her input valuable? Be open to her suggestions? A moment later, someone asked Bethany a question, and then others joined in with more inquiries. By the end of the meeting, with her help, the group had developed a revised plan that was manageable.

As Bethany and Nick walked to the exit, Aunt Ginny caught up with them.

"Oh, sweetie, I'm so proud of you. That was the best planning meeting we've had so far. And the committee members seemed very impressed."

"That's good news, Aunt Ginny. I'm glad my input was useful."

"It sure was. I think they all realize we need professional help to make our festival successful." She gave Bethany a pointed look. "Tell me honestly. Even if we hire someone, do you think it's possible to pull this off?"

"I do," Bethany replied. "But the schedule is extremely tight. The committee needs to make a commitment within the next few days and get a manager on board as soon as possible."

"But the schedule's manageable, right? Something you could handle."

"I've encountered situations like this before. It'd be tricky, but not impossible. A good event planner can make it work."

"Great. I was hoping you'd say that." Beaming, Aunt Ginny grasped Bethany's hands. "I'll get with Henry and see if he can expedite a request to hire a festival manager." She swept Bethany into an embrace. "This is so exciting. I'm going to ask him now."

As Aunt Ginny hurried off to find the town council chair, Nick turned to Bethany. "I get the impression it's going to take a lot of work to make this festival a success. Are you interested in applying for the job?"

She looked up, meeting his eyes with hers. "It'd be a challenge."

He held her gaze. "You'd never be bored."

"I'd be starting from scratch."

He stepped toward her. "You'd have lots of help."

"I'm more of a tourist than a local."

He grasped her hands. "I know a great tour guide."

"You make it hard to say *no*."

He flashed a wide smile and pulled her closer. "That's because I want you to say *yes*."

"You've given me a lot to think about."

"Good. I'm also available to eliminate doubts."

"In that case, want to grab a nightcap at Ridgely's?

I hear it's one of the oldest taverns on the Eastern Shore. People even say it's haunted. And, if I recall, I owe you a rain check."

"Absolutely." He tucked her arm around his. "But I'd like to make a stop along the way."

****

Streetlights illuminated the dark evening sky as Nick led Bethany along the sidewalk. They passed the Toasted Bean and strolled along Main Street until Ridgely Park came into view. Strains of pop music drifted out of Ridgely's Tavern as he steered her to a bench in front of the fountain. The same bench they'd shared ten years ago.

"Do you remember the last time we were here?" he asked, wrapping his hand around hers.

She nodded, her heart racing at the memory. "I wished for my first romantic kiss, and that it would be with you."

"Me too." He gently rubbed his thumb over her fingers. "It took me years to work up the courage to actually kiss you. That's why I wanted to stop at the fountain that night. To see if the maiden would make my wish come true. And when you kissed me, I felt like the luckiest guy in the world."

Nick retrieved three quarters from his pocket and flipped them, one after the other, into the pool.

"You made another wish," Bethany said, watching the ripples oscillate along the water's surface.

He reclaimed her hand, once more lacing his fingers with hers. "Three wishes, actually."

"Three? That's very ambitious."

"I couldn't stop at one because they're all important."

"What did you wish for?"

"If I tell you, it could jinx the whole process and they might not come true." He lifted her hand to his lips and lightly kissed it. "I don't know if it's worth the risk."

"I don't think the maiden is listening."

He laughed. "Okay, but don't tell anyone. First, I wished for the council to offer you the festival manager's job. The second wish is that you accept it. Because then my third wish—that you'll stay in Worthington Cove—will come true." Nick clasped their entwined fingers with his free hand and pulled Bethany even closer. "But the last thing I want is to pressure you. Leaving your home and friends to move across the country is a big decision."

She tightened her fingers around his. "When I came here, I realized something was missing from my life. Joy, maybe, or passion. A deep connection with someone. I never had that in Oklahoma City, even when I was engaged. And then yesterday, in the root cellar, you said you wanted to give whatever is happening between us a chance. Well, I do, too. I want to sit on this bench with you and wish on coins we throw in the fountain. I want to eat picnic lunches on your sailboat, and steam crabs on your pier." She paused, watching the water flow from the maiden's urn to the coin-laden water below.

"The thing is," she continued, "fear keeps holding me back. I'm afraid of moving out of my comfort zone into a situation that's new and uncertain. But I want to be bold and embrace this opportunity. Because nothing is missing when I'm with you, Nick Dorsey."

He gathered her into his arms, and she relaxed into the warmth of his body as he kissed the top of her head. Neither spoke as they clung to each other. And then Nick interrupted the quiet.

"As much as I want to banish your doubts, that's something only you can do." He reached into his pocket, retrieved a folded piece of wrapping paper, and slipped it into her hand. "But I will be here for you and provide whatever support you need while you work things through."

She opened the package. Inside was a gold ring with five tiny hearts adorning the slender band.

"Oh, Nick. It's beautiful!"

"It's the promise ring I bought for you after Natalie passed away. I kept it, hoping one day I'd have the chance to let you know my heart still belongs to you."

Bethany slipped the ring onto her finger and wrapped her arms around his waist. Then, with eyes closed, she leaned her head against his shoulder and breathed in his scent. This was how she envisioned her life in Worthington Cove. Safe, cared for, and happy. The pathway to that life was within reach. All she had to do was take it.

"Do you have another coin?" she asked.

Still holding her, Nick reached into his pocket and pulled out a quarter. She let go of him long enough to toss it into the pool.

"What did you wish for?"

"You want me to tell you and jinx the whole process?"

He snickered, then pressed his lips against her forehead. "That's okay. You don't have to. I have a feeling I know what you wished for. And if I'm right, I think our wishes have a good chance of coming true."

****

Later, in her room, Bethany settled into the upholstered chair next to the fireplace. As she watched the flames flicker and flare, the day's events overtook her thoughts.

She grieved for Samuel—for the shocking circumstances of his death, as well as the life he hadn't been able to live. The story of his suspicious death would probably make the headlines in Worthington Cove, but there would be no reparation for him aside from a footnote added to the town's historic records. She hoped it would be enough to bring closure to his spirit so he could finally rest in peace.

When the fire had burned down to embers, she slid into bed and burrowed beneath the heavy quilts. Comfort from the love of friends and family washed over her, and she was grateful for the warmth and security she felt. This truly was her home.

"Have you decided what the future holds for you, Miss Bethany?"

Samuel! He's still here!

Her eyes flew open to find him sitting on the edge of the bed. His hand rested on his thigh, drawing her gaze to the signet ring on his index finger. The initial engraved on the gold bezel was barely discernible. She glanced at his face. It radiated affection, and she couldn't help but smile in response.

"You're here. I'm really glad, but—"

"You thought that once my soul relinquished its turmoil, I would be bound for heaven?"

"Yeah, I suppose you could say that." Something about him was different. His eyes seemed brighter, less stressed. He looked almost happy.

"That doesn't appear to be my destiny."

"What do you mean?" She sat up and tugged the quilts closer to her chin to fend off the chill in the air.

"Miss Bethany, spending these last few days with you and Mr. Dorsey in the root cellar led me to reassess my circumstances." He repositioned himself on the bed. "While I am extremely grateful to you both for locating my earthly remains and recovering my ring, I realized my pursuit here is incomplete."

She frowned. "There's something else you want to do?"

He laid his hand on the quilts covering her forearm. "My life was taken from me when I was thirty-six years old. I never saw my children reach adulthood, nor was I afforded the chance to meet my grandchildren. With that said, I've been presented with a miracle. The opportunity to connect with you and Mr. Dorsey—my family." The corners of his mouth lifted into a slight smile, although his eyes remained somber. "I've grown quite fond of you both. So much so that I am quite loath to leave you. Therefore, I plan to stay."

"Here?" She blinked in surprise. "At Horatio House?"

"This house is my home. And now that I've become acquainted with you and Mr. Dorsey, I certainly can't imagine myself existing anywhere else. However, I have a request for you, as my descendant, and I ardently hope you'll honor my wish."

He has a wish? Despite the blankets covering her, Bethany shivered at his words. "I can try. What's your request?"

"I know in my heart that this town is your home, too. So, I ask that you reside in Worthington Cove. It would mean the world to me to be a part of your life, as well as the lives of your future children and grandchildren." He paused, holding her gaze. "Also, I am certain Mr. Dorsey desires your presence here as well. He's an admirable suitor. A man who has earned my highest regard. And, should you consider sharing your life with him, he would be very lucky indeed."

"Nick is pretty amazing. And I love Worthington Cove. But moving—"

"Will undoubtedly ensure your future happiness. I have no doubts that you possess the strength necessary to establish a new life here, Miss Bethany. None of the hurdles you mentioned previously are insurmountable." He leaned forward, lightly kissed her forehead, then stood. "The challenge for you is taking the leap."

Chapter 20: Taking the Leap

Bethany walked into the kitchen as Mrs. Snowden pulled a tray of muffins out of the oven. Nick was already at the dinette table, sipping coffee.

He looked up and grinned. "Hi there."

Bethany smiled, then headed to the coffeemaker. "You're here early."

"The sheriff's deputy came this morning to look at Samuel's remains in the root cellar. I took the day off in case she has more questions."

"I'm relieved we found him." She slid into the chair next to Nick. "Although the discovery is distressing, it confirms his story of what he endured that night. And it's…well, it's heart-wrenching."

Nick reached over and grasped her hand. "At least we now know the truth. And hopefully, his spirit is at peace."

"I believe it is, but not in the way we imagined."

Mrs. Snowden set a plate of muffins on the table and studied Bethany. "What do you mean, dear?"

"Samuel is still here."

Mrs. Snowden leaned in, her eyes shining with excitement. "Did he appear in a dream last night?"

Bethany nodded. "He told me he plans to remain at Horatio House." She paused, her gaze fixed on Nick. "And he had a request for me."

"What was it?"

"To stay in Worthington Cove. He wants to spend more time with me…and you, too. Since he lost his life as a fairly young man, he didn't have the chance to watch his children grow up or meet his grandchildren. Now he wants to experience that by being a part of his descendants' lives."

Nick peered at her hesitantly. "What did you say?"

"That staying here would require me to make major changes." She maintained eye contact with Nick as she continued. "And then he said something that, believe it or not, helped me put things into perspective. He told me I was strong enough to make a new life here. I just need to take the first step."

"You *are* strong enough, Bethany. But it has to be something you want to do."

She tightened her fingers around his. As she started to reply, Aunt Ginny opened the back door and stepped inside. She scanned the kitchen, then rushed over to embrace Bethany. Her face gleamed. "I have wonderful news to share."

Chuckling, Mrs. Snowden set a mug of coffee in front of Aunt Ginny. "I can tell you're about to burst. Better tell her quick!"

"Henry called an emergency town council meeting this morning to approve funding for a festival manager. The council vote was unanimous, and the planning committee now has the authority to hire someone." Beaming, Aunt Ginny sipped her coffee. "Last night, the committee members stayed on to discuss who we want to manage the festival—and everyone wants you for the job, Bethany!"

"She's right about that, dear," Mrs. Snowden said. "Your suggestions and input were just what we needed.

We never could have come up with such a good plan on our own."

"And you know the heart and soul of Worthington Cove," Aunt Ginny added. "It's easy to research the town's history, but it takes more than reading a book to understand the town's personality. Obviously, you do, which makes you the best person to take on this position."

"Congratulations!" Nick shot her a smile that illuminated his dark eyes. "My first wish came true," he said, his quiet words intended for her ears only. "Can we make it three for three?"

"We want you to start right away," Aunt Ginny continued. "Can you stop by Henry's office this morning so he can provide all the details?"

Bethany gaped at her aunt, stunned that the committee had moved so quickly to create the position *and* offer it to her. An awkward stillness fell over the kitchen, and her heart pumped frantically as she scanned the three faces watching her.

"Oh, honey," Aunt Ginny said, breaking the silence. "I'm sure Henry won't mind if you take a day or two to think about it."

Bethany focused on Nick. Being with him felt right. No matter where she landed, he was worth the leap. "I don't need a day or two." She smiled at Nick. "This is where I belong, in Worthington Cove."

"Thank god!" Nick popped out of his chair and pulled Bethany into an embrace. "I'm here for you, no matter what you need," he murmured as he nuzzled the top of her head. "Just think of me as Nick Dorsey, moral support specialist and relocation consultant."

She laughed, knowing she was making the right

choice. As she leaned up and kissed his cheek, a wisp of cold air swirled into the kitchen. Bethany felt the weight of icy fingers on her shoulders, and a moment later, Samuel's voice seeped into her consciousness.

"Welcome home, Miss Bethany."

Chapter 21: Epilogue

Behind his stone cottage, Bethany and Nick sat on the pier that reached into the Chesapeake Bay. Although the midmorning sun was bright, a November chill hung in the air. They shared a thick lap quilt as they huddled side by side at the wooden picnic table. Steam from their mugs swirled upward, carrying the aroma of freshly brewed coffee. On the table in front of them was a folded copy of the *Kent Island Beacon* that someone had left in his mailbox.

Nick opened the newspaper, and a white envelope addressed to Bethany fell onto the table. She picked up the envelope, tore open the top edge, and withdrew a sheet of ivory stationery.

"It's from Mrs. Snowden."

"Aunt Margaret wrote you a note? What'd she say?"

Bethany read the note aloud:

Dear Bethany,

You and Nick made front-page headlines! Here's a copy of the paper. I wanted to make sure you saw the article.

I'm so glad you visited Worthington Cove and stayed at Horatio House. I never dreamed your one-week getaway to our little town would result in a permanent stay, but having you here is a blessing for all of us.

When you and Nick found Samuel's ring, you two solved a mystery we didn't even know existed. Because of your perseverance, we discovered what really transpired when he was declared lost at sea. Now we know why he haunts this house. Poor man. I'm forever grateful to the both of you for bringing the truth about his death to light.

And I'm happy that Samuel is still here. I feel his presence—the guests do, too—but his mood is different. Much calmer, I think, and happier. I'm certain the discovery of his remains brought his spirit closure. When the university returns them, we'll give him a quiet burial in the family cemetery. I hope he continues to stay with us once he's been properly interred.

Please stop by soon for coffee and pastry. I'd love to see you, and I know Samuel would, too.

Love,

Margaret Snowden

Smiling, Bethany placed the note back into the envelope and snuggled against Nick. "I'm grateful, too. For Samuel. If it wasn't for him, I'd probably be back in Oklahoma City, alone and miserable."

"Wait. What about me?"

She grinned and wrapped her fingers around his. "Oh, I'm definitely grateful for you. After all, you pestered me to tell you about my dreams with Samuel, dragged me to the root cellar, and made me rake through the dirt hunting for his remains. You were relentless."

"Which was a win-win for all of us." He leaned over and lightly kissed her cheek. "Especially for me."

"I didn't fare too badly, either." She picked up the newspaper. "Here's the article your aunt was talking about. Want me to read it to you?"

He nodded. "Please."

Bethany took another sip of coffee and began:

Colonial Remains Discovered at Historic Bed-and-Breakfast

At a historic tobacco plantation in Worthington Cove, a team of forensic anthropologists from Queen Anne's University excavated skeletal remains believed to date back to the American Revolutionary War.

On October 24, Nicholas Dorsey and Bethany Hendren discovered a skeleton buried in a root cellar near Horatio House, a bed-and-breakfast on the Dorsey estate. The inn is a renovation of the plantation's original main house.

According to Dorsey, he and Hendren unearthed a human finger bone while digging in the underground structure for pottery shards and arrowheads. Dorsey added that he stopped digging immediately after the discovery and contacted the local police, as well as the anthropology department at Queen Anne's University.

"Since my family has a long history here that dates to the mid-1700s," he said, "we knew to contact the historical society if we found something that could be historically important."

She stopped and bumped her shoulder against his. "Nice quote, Dorsey."

"I sound very knowledgeable, right?"

"Yeah. But pottery shards? It makes us sound like total geeks."

"Well, I wasn't going to tell that reporter we were ghost hunting. I made an executive decision…to sound geeky rather than looney."

Laughing, Bethany continued to read:

According to Dr. Rosamund Crens, assistant professor and forensic anthropologist with Queen Anne's University, researchers at the university used various methods, such as x-rays, CT scans, and DNA analysis, to examine the skeletal remains and determine information such as the person's gender, race, height, age, and time elapsed since death.

"The skeleton from Worthington Cove is an exciting discovery," Crens said. "Our initial evaluation tells us this is a male skeleton of European descent, in his mid to late thirties, who died during the late eighteenth century. We noticed a mark on one of his ribs indicative of a stab wound from a knife, sword, or similar type of weapon. The injury more than likely caused his death."

She added that her team discovered several artifacts with the skeletal remains, including a gold signet ring; pieces of cloth woven from hemp and flax, which were used in the American colonies to make garments; and a hunting knife.

Bethany paused again. "I still can't believe Frederick Howard had the presence of mind to bury the hunting knife with Samuel."

"Right? And he must have fabricated the ship captain's letter, too. I don't think he was a particularly honorable guy."

"Me either. Thank god we're not *his* descendants."

Bethany shuddered and turned back to the newspaper, continuing to read:

"Based on our evaluation and the accompanying artifacts, we believe the remains are those of Samuel Watts, the plantation owner who lived in Horatio House with his wife Ariella Worthington Watts from 1764 until his disappearance in 1774, when he was presumed lost at sea," Crens said. "The Dorsey family owns a portrait of Samuel Watts, which shows him wearing the ring found with the remains. The signet ring strongly supports

our conclusions."

Margaret Snowden, the Horatio House innkeeper, said the discovery sheds new light on Watts' disappearance and expects the Worthington family's history will include an annotation with this latest finding.

Once the researchers complete their examination, Watts' remains will be interred in the Worthington family cemetery at the request of his descendants.

Nick grinned at Bethany when she'd finished reading. "I think Samuel's spirit is content and actually enjoys haunting the inn. Aunt Margaret says the cold drafts are much more frequent, but the guests aren't complaining. She tells them it's all part of the haunted inn experience and they love it. In fact, Samuel's getting quite famous. Everyone wants to encounter the spirit of the man who was murdered and hidden in the root cellar."

Chuckling, Bethany leaned her head against his shoulder and watched the waves lap against the sand on the little strip of beach. "I get it. Sensing his presence is thrilling. But I miss seeing him in my dreams."

"You can always spend a night or two in the Howard Room." He pulled her closer and nuzzled her hair. "I know the innkeeper. Maybe I can get you a discounted rate."

"If anyone can, it's you." She turned so that her lips brushed his. "I trust you completely."

"And I will never let you down," he said as he captured her mouth with his.

A word about the author...

Lori Matsourani is a romance addict. Give her stories with a touch of heartbreak and a spark of joy, and she's happy. Throw in characters with a huge helping of heart and soul, and she's up reading all night in romance heaven!

While currently a Texas resident, Lori grew up near Baltimore and often draws on the historical flavor of Annapolis and Maryland's Eastern Shore to inspire her story settings. She authored her first fiction story at twelve and has been hooked on writing ever since. Early on, her writing career focused on articles for magazines and newspapers before shifting to her first writing love—fiction. For Lori, connecting words to tell a story is like assembling a jigsaw puzzle, and she loves the challenge of creating every piece.

https://lorimatsourani.com

Thank you for purchasing
this publication of The Wild Rose Press, Inc.

For questions or more information
contact us at
info@thewildrosepress.com.

The Wild Rose Press, Inc.
www.thewildrosepress.com